MW01194537

*Follow the lives and loves of a complex family
with a rich history and deep ties
in the Lone Star State*

FORTUNE'S HIDDEN TREASURES

A new branch of the Fortune family
heads to idyllic Emerald Ridge to solve a
decades-long mystery that died with their
parents, and a mysterious loss that upends
their lives. Little do they know that their hearts
will never be the same!

HIS FAMILY FORTUNE

When single mom Antonia Leonetti finds out
that her fiancé's a deadbeat philanderer, her
heartbreak is compounded by humiliation:
it's none other than her family nemesis, venture
capitalist Roth Fortune, who breaks the awful
news! For years, the seemingly impenetrable
Roth has been exasperating her family with his
refusal to relinquish the neighboring vineyard
her family covets...but now he's making *Antonia*
wild—in more ways than one!

Dear Reader,

I love a mystery. And in *Fortune's Hidden Treasures*, Roth Fortune and his family have not one but two to investigate. They've come to their summer home in Emerald Ridge, Texas, to search for a special surprise hidden by their late parents twenty years ago and to help solve the mystery of what happened to a childhood friend there.

But for Roth, there's a third mystery to clear up. Just what the heck is going on with his sudden attraction to Antonia Leonetti, a woman he has no business being attracted to? For one thing, she's a business rival. For another, she's a single mom—of a toddler, no less. The last thing Roth has time for in his hectic life is a family. He doesn't know the first thing about kids. Or relationships. That's just ridiculous.

Even more ridiculous, though, is just how much he enjoys being with Antonia *and* her little girl. Talk about a mystery. Maybe, though, that's at least one of the three facing him that he could possibly solve...?

Happy reading!

Elizabeth

HIS FAMILY FORTUNE

ELIZABETH BEVARLY

THE FORTUNES OF TEXAS

If you purchased this book without a cover you should be aware that this book is stolen property. It was reported as "unsold and destroyed" to the publisher, and neither the author nor the publisher has received any payment for this "stripped book."

Special thanks and acknowledgment are given to
Elizabeth Bevarly for her contribution to
The Fortunes of Texas: Fortune's Hidden Treasures miniseries.

Harlequin®
THE FORTUNES OF TEXAS

Recycling programs
for this product may
not exist in your area.

ISBN-13: 978-1-335-14325-9

His Family Fortune

Copyright © 2025 by Harlequin Enterprises ULC

All rights reserved. No part of this book may be used or reproduced in any manner whatsoever without written permission.

Without limiting the author's and publisher's exclusive rights, any unauthorized use of this publication to train generative artificial intelligence (AI) technologies is expressly prohibited.

This is a work of fiction. Names, characters, places and incidents are either the product of the author's imagination or are used fictitiously. Any resemblance to actual persons, living or dead, businesses, companies, events or locales is entirely coincidental.

For questions and comments about the quality of this book, please contact us at CustomerService@Harlequin.com.

TM and ® are trademarks of Harlequin Enterprises ULC.

Harlequin Enterprises ULC
22 Adelaide St. West, 41st Floor
Toronto, Ontario M5H 4E3, Canada
www.Harlequin.com

Printed in Lithuania

MIX
Paper | Supporting
responsible forestry
FSC® C021394

Elizabeth Bevarly is the *New York Times* and *USA TODAY* bestselling author of more than eighty books. She has called home such exotic places as Puerto Rico and New Jersey but now lives outside her hometown of Louisville, Kentucky, with her husband and cat. When she's not writing or reading, she enjoys cooking, tending her kitchen garden and feeding the local wildlife. Visit her at elizabethbevarly.com for news and lots of fun stuff.

Visit the Author Profile page
at Harlequin.com for more titles.

For Gail Chasan and Susan Litman,

With many thanks and much gratitude.

Y'all are the best!

Prologue

"Linc Banning is dead."

Roth Fortune was barely in the front door of his family's summer home in Emerald Ridge, Texas, when his younger sister Zara told him the news. He was the last to arrive for their extended family weekend, having had to tie up some loose ends at work that morning—despite it being Saturday—before he could make the hour-long drive east from Dallas. He hadn't even had a chance yet to say hello to the rest of his family. Hell, he hadn't even said hello to Zara, who was still holding the front door open behind him.

"What do you mean?" he asked, a part of him certain he must have misheard. "We were just talking about Linc at dinner last night. How can he be…?"

Roth couldn't even think the word. Growing up, Linc Banning had been the son of the Fortune family's housekeeper Delia, but he and his mother both might as well have been members of the Fortune family, so close had they all been. Although Linc had been six years Roth's junior, he was nearly the same age as their sister Priscilla and only a couple years younger than Zara. Even with the age difference, though, Roth and his younger-by-a-year brother, Harris, had taken the kid under their wing, filling him in on all the arcane stuff teenage boys passed along to their prepubescent counterparts. Like how to spin a curveball and hold a girl's hand without getting sweaty palms. Linc *couldn't* be dead. He'd been too full of life when they were kids.

"He was murdered," Zara added, her green eyes going damp with tears.

At that, Roth actually dropped the weekender bag he'd been holding. It fell with a thump onto the floor, a sound punctuated by a soft sniffle coming from the living room. When he looked that way, he saw his other siblings and his cousin Kelsey and uncle Sander in various states of distress and disbelief.

"They found his body in the river last night," Priscilla said from behind the tissue pressed to her nose. "While we were all laughing it up over pork rillettes and crab Oscar at Talia 469 in Dallas last night, Linc was being shot through the chest."

Roth shook his head in disbelief. Who would kill Linc? And *why*? Although it was true that he and the rest of the Fortunes had kind of lost touch with the guy after Delia Banning's death five years ago, they'd still seen him around town occasionally whenever they visited Emerald Ridge. And if Linc had seemed to be avoiding them every time they did, they'd all just figured it might be because the guy was embarrassed that he had yet to accomplish all the things he'd dreamed of by now. Such as having his own mansion like this one, for instance, and a private plane like the one Roth's parents, Mark and Marlene, had owned…and died in twenty years ago this month. Then again, it had been so long since any of them really talked to Linc that, for all any of them knew, he *had* achieved those goals and was avoiding them for a different reason entirely.

All Linc's *When I grow up, I'm gonna be rich like you guys* stuff had just been talk when they were kids. Who cared what Linc had or hadn't achieved by now? He was always a good guy. The last person on earth anyone would want to murder.

"Right now, we don't know too many details," his brother, Harris, said. "Only what we've heard from a few people in town, which may or may not even be reliable info. I'm sure the cops will want to talk to us. Maybe not yet since we just arrived today, but they'll probably come by for a chat before too long."

And what were they supposed to tell them? Roth wondered. That they didn't even know what Linc had been doing for a living these days? Or where he'd even hung his hat here in town lately?

"I don't understand," Roth said. "Who would want to kill Linc?"

"That's what we'd all like to know," Kelsey chimed in softly.

Sander nodded. "Yeah. Us and everybody else in Emerald Ridge." His expression turned stonier than Roth had ever seen it, somehow making him look far older than his forty-four years. "I know we originally planned to just be in town for the weekend to pay tribute to your folks and look for that long-lost 'surprise' they buried here, but... Roth, we did some talking before you got here. And we all decided that we're not going anywhere until we have some answers about Linc."

His head still spinning, Roth nodded. "Then I'm not going anywhere, either."

Chapter One

"I still can't believe you and Linc went out together last month and you didn't even tell any of us about it."

Roth Fortune eyed his sister Priscilla with mock severity as he lifted his coffee for a sip. The two of them had escaped a chaotic Saturday morning at the family's summer compound in Emerald Ridge, Texas, to grab an early lunch at a popular eatery in town. Located off the lobby of the Emerald Ridge Hotel, the café was homey and comfortable, from its pale yellow walls to its blue checkered tablecloths to the brightly painted pots spilling all manner of greenery. Old-school country music played faintly in the background—currently segueing from Merle Haggard to Patsy Cline—and the air was heavy with the aroma of freshly baked pastries. After finishing their sandwiches, they'd had no choice but to succumb to the fragrances of cinnamon and cardamom and had ordered a basket of churros, now half-empty, to split for dessert.

Priscilla halted the motion one of those churros had been making to her mouth and eyed Roth right back. Her long blond hair was bound in a loose ponytail, and her hazel eyes flashed with clear irritation at his comment. Although she was twenty-eight, there was a part of Roth that would always see her as the little girl she was when their parents perished in that plane crash over the San Bernardino Mountains of Southern California all those years ago. It was a tragedy that had forever changed the trajectory of all their lives.

Roth sighed. His sister probably thought he *had* spoken the comment as if she were a child, and yeah, okay, maybe that had been in his tone. He would doubtless always see his three siblings as little kids. Even though he'd pretty much been a kid himself when Mark and Marlene died—and their uncle Sander had stepped up immediately to care for them after that—Roth was the oldest. And the oldest always watched out for his family, no matter what.

"Okay, for *one thing*," Priscilla began, "I don't have to tell you everything I do, even if you did make yourself a de facto parent to the rest of us after we lost Mom and Dad."

"I did not make myself a de facto—"

"And *two*," she interrupted, since that was an old argument, and her point was also kinda true, "it was only one date. That Linc and I didn't even realize was going to turn into a date. It was supposed to just be a quick catch-up after running into each other in town. Until the big surprise kiss at the end, anyway. Then he ghosted me after that, so…"

She tossed the churro back into the basket and reached for her iced tea.

"The whole thing was just so weird. Not only the kiss, which came out of nowhere, but why would he text me mere hours after a nice evening like that and tell me he can't see me anymore—" she lifted her hands to make air quotes with her fingers "'—for my own good'? And then block me? We'd even made plans to go out again the next night."

Priscilla had dropped the bomb about her single date with Linc the afternoon Roth arrived for what was supposed to have been a long weekend in Emerald Ridge. In on Saturday, the second of August, out on Monday the fourth. That was how it was supposed to have been. But now, in light of what had happened, the family had decided they were going to stay at least until Labor Day, something that wasn't exactly going to be conducive to running his business an hour away in Dallas. But family came first, and Linc Banning had always been like a member of the Fortune family. Well, at least until Priscilla's revelation about going out with him after running into him last month when she was here visiting a childhood friend.

When she'd told the rest of the family about the encounter, they'd all decided pretty quickly that she needed to tell the local police, too. So they'd all marched down to the sheriff's office where she (a) was able to volunteer the revelation first and (b) presented her alibi in the form of the four-hour-long dinner the family had been enjoying an hour away in Dallas when Linc was killed. Now, a week later, just about everything regarding Linc's murder was up in the air, and practically anyone in town could be a suspect. Except, thankfully, for the lately arrived Fortunes.

Priscilla ran an errant finger around the rim of her

glass. "And we've been hearing all this stuff about him that doesn't sound anything like the Linc we used to know."

It was true. Roth himself had heard some of the locals talking about how Linc had made some enemies here in Emerald Ridge recently, but no one seemed to know the source of the animosity, and couldn't even pinpoint exactly who these supposed enemies were. Typical gossip stuff. But the more he'd heard over the last week about Linc and his recent comings and goings here in Emerald Ridge, the bigger the mystery around his murder became.

"I know," he agreed. "But I can't believe Linc would be involved in anything that would lead to someone killing him. Then again, none of us except you has really even spoken to him for years. Not more than a few words anyway."

"And I only spoke to him at length that one night," Priscilla said. "But he seemed fine. Like the Linc we've always known and loved. I mean, maybe a little preoccupied at times, but that was understandable, since we hadn't talked that in depth for so long. There was nothing that made me think he was in trouble or anything."

"You sure he didn't say or do anything out of the ordinary?"

"Nope." She shook her head. "We had a great time."

"And then he ghosted you."

Now she nodded.

"Which is out of the ordinary if you think about it. He never would have done something like that under normal circumstances."

"Good point."

Roth ran a restless hand through his dark brown hair and leaned back in his chair, crossing his arms over the pinstriped camp shirt he'd paired with the only pair of jeans he'd brought with him to Emerald Ridge. Okay, the only pair of jeans he owned. Sure, there were some venture capitalists out there who did business from home in cargo shorts and *Fortnite* T-shirts. Not him. His favorite professor-mentor at UT Austin had been one of the sharpest-dressed men he'd ever met, and he'd commanded respect on sight with his trademark bespoke suits. Roth had adopted the style himself after graduating, feeling like a million bucks long before he actually earned his first million. To this day, he kept a professional office in Uptown Dallas and a personal tailor downtown. And, of course, he owned an impressive collection of Stetsons. His favorite, a fawn-colored Monterey, currently occupied the seat beside him.

"Did Linc tell you what he's been up to lately?" he asked his sister. "What he's been doing since his mother's death? How he's made his living? Where he was staying? Anything?"

She shook her head again. "I don't even know for sure if he was an Emerald Ridge resident. He could have just been visiting, too."

Linc and his mother had lived with the Fortunes in Dallas when they were kids, and had followed them to Emerald Ridge every summer, so Delia could keep the house for them here, too. After Delia's death five years ago, Linc had struck out on his own, talking a big game about how he was going to make his way in the world, along with millions, maybe even billions, of dollars, and how the next time any of the Fortunes saw him, he was going to be living the high life the same way they did. All of them had run into him in some capacity or other since then, usually here in Emerald Ridge, but none of them had ever been able to pin him down long enough to find out where he was living, or how, exactly, he was getting along. It sounded to Roth now like that had still been the case when he and Priscilla went out last month.

She looked thoughtful. "Now that you mention it, though, he didn't really say much about himself at all that night. We mostly talked about me, because he kept asking me questions about what I was doing and how everyone else in the family was."

"Maybe he was just trying to get closer to you to get his hands on the Fortune fortune," Roth half joked in light of Linc's interest in the rest of the family. Although that didn't sound like the decent guy he remembered.

Priscilla expelled a sound of derision. "Yeah, well, that might be the case if *he* hadn't been the one to dump *me*," she pointed out.

True enough.

She sighed. "I guess all we can do now is what we decided to do a week ago. Hang around town, see what happens and help with the investigation however we can. I'm just glad everyone's in a place right now where we can afford to take time to do that."

Speak for yourself, Roth wanted to say. Although he could work remotely just fine for a little while, and Dallas was only an hour away if something pressing came up that needed his personal attention, he didn't like being physically away from the office. He spent more time there than he did at home. Hell, there were times when Fortune Capital was more of a home to him than the massive Victory Park condo he'd bought two years ago and had yet to finish furnishing. Who needed more than a bed, a fridge and a microwave when you were too busy to do anything more than sleep, eat and go to the office?

Priscilla smiled. "If nothing else, the longer stay will at least give us more time to find Mom and Dad's long-lost family surprise."

Which was the other reason the six surviving Fortunes had come to Emerald Ridge this month. In addition to commemorating the twentieth anniversary of Mark and Marlene's deaths, the family wanted to look for that age-old hidden treasure their parents had stashed somewhere in or around their summer home. Before the elder Fortunes left for their fateful trip—they'd been going to the West Coast to look at a minor league baseball team they were thinking about buying—they had told their children about a wonderful surprise they'd hidden somewhere on their Emerald Ridge property, and how much fun the kids would have looking for it. They'd assured Roth and his siblings they'd give them some hints to get them started when they returned. But then tragedy struck, and the whereabouts of the secret gift remained a mystery.

For the last two decades, every summer until the last few—they all had busy lives as adults, after all—the family had done their best to vacation together in Emerald Ridge, upholding the tradition their parents started before they were even born. And every time they'd been here, they'd searched for whatever this hidden family surprise might be. But with a huge summer mansion, four mini-mansion guesthouses that each of the siblings was living in for now—Sander and Kelsey were staying at the main house—and a boathouse and dock, not to mention dozens of acres of land, they'd never found a trace of anything. It would have helped if they'd even known what they were looking for, but with no further clues from their parents, it could be anything, of any size, and it could be *anywhere*.

Before he could reply, Priscilla changed the subject. "So now that you know how my own love life isn't going so well—the more things change, the more they stay the same—how's yours? Are you and Grace still seeing each other?"

Roth hadn't seen Grace for months, not since she started talking about what a wonderful father he would be after he'd introduced her to his family the first—and only—time. For one thing, Roth, workaholic that he was, would be a terrible father—no way was he going to procreate. And for another thing, he and Grace had been dating less than six months at that point. Envisioning him as a father was the last thing she should have been doing after such a short time. But she'd kept building some picket-fence fantasy every time they were together, right down to telling him how happy she was going to be when she could take a sabbatical from being a financial analyst to bake cookies as a stay-at-home mom instead.

Yeah, no.

"Grace and I are taking a break," he told Priscilla diplomatically.

Priscilla raised one blond brow in an all-too-familiar way.

"Fine," Roth conceded. "She and I broke up."

His sister looked in no way surprised. "That's three breakups in less than two years," she said. "What was it this time? She wanted the two of you to be exclusive?" Then she answered her own question. "No, that was Min. You couldn't at least make a verbal commitment? Oh sorry, that was Anjali. So what *was* it with Grace? She couldn't possibly have been expecting a ring so soon."

At Roth's sound of frustration, Priscilla gaped. "She was already talking marriage?"

"She was already talking about running for PA president at our children's—yes, more than one—fictional school."

"Wow," Priscilla said. "That's a new one, even for a master womanizer like you."

"I am not a master womanizer," he denied. He had years yet before he could be called that. Right now, he was just sort of a semi-pro. "But I admit that women in Dallas *and* Emerald Ridge don't think too kindly of me these days because I can't commit."

"Can't or don't want to?" his sister asked.

What's the difference? Roth wanted to counter. Besides, he'd made commitments. Kind of. One of his exes had even told him *she* was breaking up with *him* because he was *too* committed. To his siblings, not to her. She'd pointed out that every time one of the other Fortunes needed something, Roth dropped everything and ran to help. He knew that wasn't true and had reminded her that he wasn't his family's caretaker, and that all four Fortune siblings had been taken in by their father's brother Sander, who was the effective head of the family—only to have her remind him right back that he and his uncle constantly butted heads to this day about how Sander had taken over, even though twenty years had passed since he did.

Blah, blah, blah. The two of them got along just fine. Usually. Okay, sometimes Sander got on his nerves, but only when he was meddling too much in their lives. Which had been his habit. For twenty years. Roth still loved and respected the guy.

Anyway.

Priscilla folded her arms on the table and looked at him with a speculative smile. "You know, someday, you're going to meet a woman who'll knock you off your feet, and you're not going to know what hit you. I just hope I'm around to see it when it happens."

Yeah, well, Roth hoped her cataracts weren't so bad by the time that happened that she missed it.

He was about to tell her that, but a loud guffaw from the table behind him drew his attention that way—again—and he clenched his jaw. Charles Cabot had come into the café not long after Roth and Priscilla sat down, and Roth had been on edge ever since. That miscreant had been Roth's Emerald Ridge nemesis since the two of them were eight years old. Ever since the day Cabot sauntered to the side of the swimming pool at the Emerald Ridge Park and oh-so-carelessly shoved five-year-old Zara into the deep end. His baby sister, who hadn't yet gotten the hang of swimming, still managed to surface, sputtering and splashing, clearly in distress. All Cabot did was point and laugh.

After Roth jumped in to pull Zara out and made sure she was okay, he'd sauntered over to Cabot and oh-so-carelessly slugged him with all the force an angry eight-year-old boy could muster. Which, at the time, had been a lot, because Cabot went into the pool, too. Right on top of Señora Cardenas—the wife of Emerald Ridge's then-mayor—taking her down with him. Cabot had spent the rest of the summer mowing the Cardenases' lawn for free every Friday, while Roth was hailed as a hero.

Last he'd heard, Cabot had been plying his trade as a smarmy, obnoxious real estate investor in Houston for the last ten years. It was naturally Roth's bad luck that they'd both be back in Emerald Ridge at the same time. Ever since his arrival at the café, Cabot had been too busy yakking at the guy with him to even notice Roth. At the moment, he was loudly winding up a story about the state of the housing market and how tough it was to make a buck these days.

Oh, boo frickin' hoo, Cabot.

The fact that he was still smarmy and obnoxious, though, was made clear within seconds, because after finishing his real estate narrative, Cabot launched into another one about Antonia Leonetti, whom Roth had seen with him around town a couple of times over the last week. The two of them were clearly dating, though what Antonia could possibly see in that jerk was beyond him.

Then again, Roth didn't know the woman well, since she was a few years younger than him, so they'd never moved in the same friend groups during the summers the Fortunes had spent in town. But from what Roth could tell, Antonia was the antithesis of Charles Cabot—elegant, articulate and beautiful, and smart enough—and a big enough shark—to be the CFO of her family's vineyard here in Emerald Ridge. He knew she was a shark, because she had also been a major thorn—or maybe a major *tooth*—in his side since he bought his own vineyard just outside of town five years ago. One the Leonettis had been certain they would eventually take over themselves…and were still trying to take over, despite Roth's years-long ownership.

To their credit, the family had, thus far, done things by the book, making him offer after offer to buy—every one of which he'd turned down. Then they'd started in with their proposals to merge the businesses, couriering to his Dallas office one tidy blue folder after another filled with documents assuring him he'd still have ownership of Fortune's Vintages but would have absolutely nothing to do with the running of the place. And, by the way, what would he think about changing the name from Fortune's Vintages to Leonetti Vintages? Or, better yet, just selling it to them, hmm?

That was not going to happen. Like, ever. The whole reason Roth had bought Fortune's Vintages to begin with was to be a part of it. No, he didn't want to be the one running the show there, but he definitely liked being involved in small ways from a distance. He'd had an interest in wine for as long as he could remember, having watched his father make it as a hobby when he was a kid. And when he'd had his first taste—a half glass on his sixteenth birthday under the watchful eye of both parents—he'd become enamored of it. The fact that something like a grape could be both a lunch bag snack for kids and a little taste of Dionysian revelry for grown-ups had fascinated him. No way was he going to sell Fortune's Vintages to the Leonettis or anyone else.

Even so, he rankled to hear Charles Cabot going on about Antonia now, especially when the guy started throwing around some less-than-flattering comments about her and talking trash about how she cared more about her kid than she did him. Roth had forgotten that, on top of everything else, Antonia was a single mother, which just made all her other accomplishments that much more impressive. What could she possibly see in a guy like Cabot?

Maybe Roth and Antonia weren't friends—to put it mildly—but he had a lot of respect for her. He'd learned enough about the wine business by now to know how competitive it was and how difficult it could be to turn a profit. Yes, Fortune's Vintages was already considered a prestigious winery among oenophiles, and with a little more work and time, it could become a huge success. Maybe not as huge as Fortune Capital—which was successful to the tune of billions of dollars—but a success nonetheless. And he was having fun with it. It was a nice counter to the high-stakes, fast-moving world of Dallas finance.

"Anyway," Priscilla was saying, bringing Roth's attention back to the matter at hand, "when you *do* eventually fall for a woman, you're going to fall *hard*."

Right. They'd been talking about how Roth couldn't make a commitment to a romantic entanglement, on account of he was too busy being noncommittal about romantic entanglements.

"What am I supposed to do?" he asked his sister. "I have a billion-dollar business to run in Dallas, and a few more smaller ones that are still fairly major investments I need to keep track of, not the least of which is Fortune's Vintages here. I'm trying to divide my time between Dallas and a handful of other places. A handful of other places, I might add, where none of the women seem to like me very much."

She bit back a smile at that. "Well, you know, if you'd make a teeny bit more of an investment in one of them, that might not be the case."

"I'm just not the kind of man women seem to want these days. I'm too ruthless and cutthroat."

Now Priscilla didn't bother to hide her amusement, erupting with a single incredulous laugh. "You? Ruthless and cutthroat? You're the biggest cinnamon roll I know."

This time Roth was the one to sputter in disbelief. "I am *not* a cinnamon roll." He was too ruthless and cutthroat. And also too pragmatic and emotionless. He'd been called those things by an ex, too.

"You can deny it as much as you want," Priscilla told him. "But I have you pegged. Deep down, you have a heart as big as Texas. It became especially obvious after Mom and Dad died. You were like a mother hen, always arguing with Sander about who was going to take care of us kids and how. And you were only thirteen at the time, making you one of the kids who needed to be taken care of in the first place."

"Sander had no idea what he was getting into," Roth grumbled. "Hell, he was only twenty-four himself."

"Meaning he knew a bit more about life than a thirteen-year-old boy. You should've been worrying about cross-country try-outs at school and zit cream, not how you were going to see to the needs of a bunch of grieving children. Not when you were one of those grieving children yourself." She smiled a little sadly now. "You big cinnamon roll."

Roth was about to argue with her—for one thing, he'd never needed zit cream—but something Cabot said behind him brought his attention back to his childhood nemesis. It was the words *Antonia* and *fiancée* and *wedding* that did it. What the…? Were Cabot and Antonia actually *engaged*?

Evidently, they were, because the next thing Cabot said to his companion was, "I'm *this* close to marrying into *aaaallll* that Leonetti money, and then I'll be back in the black."

His companion chuckled a little nervously, then reminded Cabot, "Yeah, but then you'll be married. Total lifestyle change for you. Gonna have to say farewell to the ladies."

Without a single hesitation, the jerk responded, "Being married doesn't mean I can't have fun. Hell, the ladies are drawn to wedding rings." He chuckled, too, but there was something in the sound that made Roth's flesh crawl. "Besides, I'll only have to put in five years, long enough to let the prenup run its course. Thank God I have a pit bull lawyer. I'll get what I want out of Antonia." He laughed his coarse laugh again. "In more ways than one. I just wish she didn't have that snot-encrusted little rug rat demanding so much of her attention. I swear that kid's nothing but a germ factory. But she's a means to an end as much as her mother is, so I have no choice but to put up with both of them for a while to get to that pot of gold."

Roth was steaming mad by the time Cabot finished. Just who the hell did he think he was, lying to and manipulating and flagrantly using a woman like Antonia for financial gain? And doing it while badmouthing both her and her daughter? The sleaze was going to marry her with the single intention of divorcing her and taking her to the cleaners financially as soon as he possibly could. While Antonia was doubtless thinking she was entering into a lifelong commitment to create a family with him and her little girl. What Cabot was planning wasn't going to wreck one life, but two, one of which was that of a helpless little kid. Antonia wouldn't marry a man like him in a million years if she knew the truth.

Jeez. Where was a swimming pool and a mayor's wife when you needed one?

Roth was about to stand up and give Cabot a piece of his mind—among other things—but the scumbag stood first, saying something to his companion about how he hadn't realized how late it had gotten, and he was due for a tuxedo fitting, so he had to bolt. Damn. The wedding date must be pretty close if he was already doing the tuxedo thing. Then Cabot was making his way to the exit, moving so quickly that Roth didn't even have a chance to stick out his foot to trip him.

He looked at his sister to see if she had overheard what he had, but she was still going on about Roth's love life—or lack thereof— and didn't seem to have heard a word Cabot had said. So Roth quickly filled her in.

"Yeah, well, consider the source," Priscilla said blandly. "Charles Cabot has always been a dirtball."

"Antonia Leonetti doesn't seem to think so."

"Antonia didn't know him that well when we were kids," Priscilla reminded him. "She was always the quiet member of the Leonetti family back then, hanging back from the rest of us. And you know Charles—he always went for the party girls who were looking for a good time the same way he was. Even so, from what I've heard, he started going after Antonia the minute he got back to town last fall, sweeping her right off her feet." She shrugged. "I just thought he'd finally grown up and was looking for someone steady now. Guess not, after what you just heard him say."

"Why hasn't anyone warned her about him?"

Priscilla shrugged. "The prevailing consensus of local gossip seems to be that he was gone for a long time and has seemed like a different man since he came back. He's been super nice and charming to everybody, but especially to Antonia. I guess everyone just thinks he's changed."

"And now he's talked her into marrying him."

Priscilla nodded. "Wedding is next month, I think."

Unbelievable, Roth thought. Antonia Leonetti was a

month away from what was going to be the biggest mistake of her life, and she didn't even realize it.

"Yeah, well, after what I just heard," he said, "the dirtbag obviously hasn't changed at all. Someone needs to tell Antonia the truth about him. Before it's too late."

At this, Priscilla looked at him as if he'd just grown a third eye. "What do you care? You and Antonia—you and all the Leonettis for that matter—have been at each other's throats ever since they made their first offer to buy Fortune's Vintages from you."

Yeah, okay, there was that, Roth thought. He'd been especially insulted by their first offer, which had been laughably low and clearly made with the opinion that he was a complete idiot. Ironically, it had been that lowball offer that had made him even more determined to make the vineyard a success. And the more successful it had become, the more aggressively the Leonettis had pursued its purchase. Roth was still doing his best to ignore them, but they were really starting to get on his nerves. Every time one of those damned blue folders showed up on his desk in Dallas, his blood pressure inched up more than a few notches. He was kind of surprised he hadn't received one of their infamous proposals since coming back to town last weekend. Then again, with a wedding looming, Antonia probably had other things on her mind.

"This isn't about Antonia and her family being the annoying owners of an even more annoying rival business," Roth told his sister. "It's about human decency."

Priscilla nodded sagely. "And cinnamon rolls like you always do the right thing."

"I am not a cinnamon—" Roth blew out an exasperated sound and left the denial unfinished. Priscilla, he could see, was enjoying his objections way too much. "Every human being should do the right thing," he said instead.

Even the ones who were ruthless and cutthroat, like him. Even the pragmatic, emotionless ones, like him. Someone needed to tell Antonia Leonetti how big a mistake she was about to make.

And Roth knew just the guy to do it.

Chapter Two

Antonia Leonetti gazed into the front window of Emerald Ridge Weddings, a tony bridal boutique in the heart of her hometown, and wondered if maybe she was making a mistake. Not about marrying Charles Cabot, of course—saying yes to his proposal two months ago was probably the most common-sense decision she'd ever made—but about the dress she'd chosen for their wedding six weeks hence.

Naturally, she hadn't gone for white, since this was her second marriage, and she was the mom of a nearly one-year-old. Nor had she opted for a poufy gown more suited to a young twentysomething than a nearly thirty-year-old. She hadn't even gone for the pouf when she married Georgie's father as a young twentysomething herself. But now, glimpsing the simple dove-gray tea-length dress in the shop's window, she was questioning the slinky ivory dress full of sparkles that she'd ultimately ordered.

She reminded herself that Charles liked glitzy-type dresses more suited to movie stars. That was why Antonia had chosen her dress in the first place. Okay, fine. That was why she'd let Charles talk her into the dress she chose. But slinky and sparkly wasn't exactly Antonia Leonetti. Simple dove gray was more her style. There was still time to change her mind, she thought. Not about marrying Charles, of course, but about the dress.

Decisions, decisions...

If only her sisters, Bella and Gia, had said yes to her invitation to join her today when she'd called them this morning to have them come along for her first fitting. They were both way savvier about current trends in fashion—and just about everything else—than she was. Give Antonia a wardrobe filled with fitted shirts and tailored trousers and pencil skirts—things that never went out of style, so she didn't have to keep track of what was fashionable—and she was fine. She had more pressing things to think about than appropriate heights for waistlines, hemlines and heels. After all, she was the CFO of a successful family business that had been around for three generations. This weekend alone, she had to finish a quarterly regulatory response report and read over some new federal tax guidelines that could have a significant impact on agricultural businesses like Leonetti Vineyards. Unfortunately, Bella and Gia had both had obligations that had prevented them from coming. Really last-minute, really lame obligations.

The truth was, neither of Antonia's sisters liked Charles, and neither of them had made a secret of that. They both thought he was slick and hard to get to know and that Antonia should wait a bit longer to make sure he was the right man to be both her husband and Georgie's father. Her brother, Leo, had been even more vocal in his misgivings about the guy, stating flat out that

Charles Cabot was a big phony pretending to be something he wasn't.

Which was ridiculous. Charles was wonderful. Otherwise, Antonia wouldn't be marrying him. Her family just didn't know him the way she did. He traveled around Texas a lot for his business, and her siblings just hadn't had the chance to get to know him as well as she did. Once they spent more time with him, they'd see he was the perfect choice for her and Georgie both.

Antonia never would have even gone out with him in the first place if he were slick or phony, since she had more than enough experience with that kind of man. She'd married the first time for love and romance and happily-ever-after and look how that had turned out. Unbeknownst to her, Silvio had started cheating on her before they even walked down the aisle, and by the time they split up, shortly after Antonia discovered she was pregnant, he had a veritable harem of women stringing from one continent to another. No way was she going to marry again for hearts and flowers when her first marriage had been anything but.

Charles was a solid guy. A *good* guy. He was as practical and common-sense as she was. Antonia was through with her old emotional, impulsive ways. She wasn't an impetuous kid anymore. She had realized immediately after starting to date Charles how down-to-earth he was. They shared the same philosophies about life and finances and family—and pretty much everything else—not to mention he was gorgeous and funny and smart. He was going to be the perfect husband and father.

So maybe she wasn't wildly in love with him. Love was overrated. She liked Charles a lot. He liked her. He'd even professed to love her. With time, she would doubtless grow to love him, too. They were both going into this marriage with eyes wide open. It was a meeting of minds as much as it was of hearts. They were both at points in their lives when it was time to settle down and get serious and make plans for the future. Antonia didn't want to spend her life alone, and she wanted Georgie to have someone in her life who would love her and be an involved father.

Pep talk over, Antonia gave the gray dress in the bridal shop window one last longing look, then wrapped her fingers around the door handle and began to pull it open. She was halted before completing the action, however, when she heard a man call out her name—her full name, Antonia Leonetti, as if whoever it was didn't know exactly which one to choose.

When she looked down the street, she saw Roth Fortune heading toward her with a strong, certain gait, as if he needed to tell her something Very Important. She couldn't imagine what it might be. The last time she'd had any contact with him, it was a terse email rejecting the Leonettis' offer to buy Fortune's Vintages and a thinly veiled threat to…do something—he hadn't exactly specified what—if she ever contacted him again. From that moment forth, he'd concluded, she and the rest of her family should instead contact his attorney instead of him, *whose credentials are included below, have a nice day.*

It was no secret in Emerald Ridge that the two of them

were, um, not exactly friendly. The fact was, though, that they barely knew each other at all. They'd probably only exchanged a few dozen words in person since they were kids, and probably even fewer than that back then. Roth and his siblings had always run around with the cool kids when they were in town during the summer— her own siblings included. Antonia had been the bookish, quiet one of the Leonettis and had kept her distance from…well, almost everyone. Roth and the rest of the Fortunes had just been too rambunctious for her liking.

He was still too rambunctious for her liking. And too cagey. Oh, and talk about *slick*; that was the very definition of Roth Fortune, who—surprise, surprise—made his millions as a venture capitalist. All those guys did was throw around other people's money for a living. And who other than a cagey, *slick* person would buy the property that would become Fortune's Vintages out from under the Leonettis—who'd had a gentleman's agreement with the previous owner—before the place even went up for sale? Then have the audacity to reject every offer the Leonettis made to buy it from him after that, as if none of their offers were fair. After blowing them all off so coolly and completely, was it any wonder the Leonettis and Roth Fortune had become adversaries?

Maybe he'd changed his mind, she thought now as he hastened his stride toward her. It had been a few months since they'd sent him their last proposal—which he'd mailed back clearly untouched with a Post-it note on the front of the blue folder that simply said *No*. But a lot of things could have changed between then and now. Maybe he needed capital for some new venture.

"Roth Fortune," she greeted him just as formally as he had her once he was within earshot. "What can I do for you?"

He came to a halt a little closer to her than she would have liked, but she didn't step back. On the contrary, she straightened to her full five foot ten, something that normally made men a little uncomfortable because she was able to look them right in the eye. Roth Fortune, however, topped six feet—and then some—so she still had to look up to him.

Dammit. Being this close also made her remember just how handsome he was.

In fact, this might be the closest she'd ever stood to him. She'd never realized what beautiful eyes he had. Even shaded by the Stetson riding low on his forehead, she could see tiny bits of green mixing with the blue in a way that rivaled the waters of the Caribbean. Coupled with his dark brown hair, his exquisitely carved cheekbones and a full mouth that made a woman want to wreak mayhem, he was way more handsome than she remembered. In fact, he was downright—

Nothing, Antonia told herself. He was downright nothing. There were a million men out there who were handsome, including her fiancé. *Especially* her fiancé. Charles. Cabot. What the heck? Why was she reminding herself of his name like that? She knew his name backward and forward. Just because Roth Fortune was standing way too close, looking way too attractive, that didn't mean she needed to remind herself whom she was marrying. Anyway, where was she…? Right. Wondering why Roth Fortune was looking for her.

As if reading her mind, he asked, "Got a minute? I need to tell you something."

Tell her something. Not ask her something. Like *ask* whether her family was still interested in buying Fortune's Vintages. She brightened. Maybe he wanted to *tell* her he was putting it up for sale.

But what he said was, "It's about your fiancé."

Certainly it was no secret in town that Antonia and Charles were getting married next month. She'd sent out save-the-date cards a month ago, and although the ceremony wasn't going to be huge, weddings were always fodder for talk in Emerald Ridge. Roth Fortune, however, didn't seem like the type of person to engage in gossip. And he and his family had barely been back in town for a week. What could he possibly have to tell her about her fiancé?

"Charles Cabot," he clarified. As if Antonia needed to be reminded whom she was marrying again.

"I know my fiancé's name," she assured him. "What about Charles?"

Roth's gaze, which had been so fixed on hers, suddenly ricocheted off onto something over her left shoulder. He shifted his weight from one foot to the other, then back again. Then he cupped his hand over the back of his nape as if he were anxious about something.

"Mr. Fortune?" she said, automatically reverting to business mode when it came to addressing a business rival.

Now his gaze flew back to hers. "Call me Roth."

His commanding tone made her want to call him

something else entirely. Instead, she remained silent, never flinching from his gaze.

He blew out an exasperated breath. "I was having lunch with my sister Priscilla at Emerald Ridge Café earlier today."

When he didn't elaborate any further, Antonia asked, "And?"

Instead of telling her something about Charles, he blurted, "Have you tried their churros by any chance? Those things are incredible."

Antonia narrowed her eyes at him. Just what the devil was going on with him? Had it not been midafternoon, she would have wondered if he'd been drinking. But he was obviously stone-cold sober. Distracted by churros, maybe, but totally sober.

"They do have good churros," she agreed. She reached for the bridal shop's door again. "Now, if you'll excuse me, if you don't have anything else to discuss, I'm late for a fitting."

"Wait," Roth said.

He lifted a hand to cover hers on the door handle, as if he wanted to physically stop her from going into the shop. Then, seeming as surprised by the gesture as she was, he threw her a look that was at once apologetic and imploring. He didn't remove his hand, though, only curled his fingers more insistently over hers. An odd thrill of something hot and electric went up Antonia's spine at the contact. But she didn't remove her hand, either.

More curious than ever now, she said, "Mr. Fortune, just what do you need to tell me about Charles?" Then another thought struck her, and she removed her hand from beneath his to turn to face him fully. "Is he okay? Was he hurt?"

Roth immediately shook his head, dropping his own hand back to his side. "No, nothing like that." His expression suddenly hardened. "But I won't say he's okay, either."

She shook her head. "What are you talking about?"

He expelled another sound of annoyance. "He and one of his friends were at the table next to me and Priscilla, and I overheard him say..." Here, the sound he emitted was more of contempt. "Some not particularly nice things."

Right. Sure. Somehow, Antonia refrained from rolling her eyes. The only times she had heard Charles badmouth anything—and there were only a few—it had been about the current real estate market. Once or twice, *maybe*, he had been irritated about a business rival or unruly client. But who wasn't peeved sometimes by people who made their life more difficult in some way? Case in point: Roth Fortune.

"What kind of bad things?" she asked. "Did he mention how high interest rates were stalling sales? How some sellers or buyers had unrealistic expectations? Oh, no. How shocking. Call Miss Manners."

"He wasn't talking about work," Roth said, his imperious tone gentling. Then he swallowed hard as if he dreaded what he was about to say next. "He was talking about you."

Antonia hated the way her stomach pitched when he said that, as if some part of her could actually believe

that Charles would speak badly about her. But her fiancé would never speak badly about her. He *loved* her.
He'd said so a million times. And even if she'd never
echoed the words back to him, on some level, she loved
Charles, too. Maybe some part of her might not be entirely on board yet, but the rest of her—the parts that
mattered, like her affections and her smarts and her
common sense—didn't have a doubt at all.

"Don't be ridiculous," she told him. "Charles would
never say anything about me that wasn't nice. You're
just trying to start trouble."

Here, Roth looked genuinely mystified. "Why would
I want to do that?"

Honestly, she had no idea. But there was no way
Charles would ever say something bad about her. "I
don't know," she replied. "But you and I—you and my
family—" she hastily corrected herself "—aren't exactly
on the best of terms."

He frowned again. "Oh, well, maybe if you and your
family stopped badgering me about selling Fortune's
Vintages and sending over your ridiculous proposals
one after another, I'd—"

"You'd what?" Antonia interjected. Was he saying
he would sell to them for the right price after all this
time telling them they'd never get their hands on the
place? That the reason he hadn't sold yet was because
they hadn't made a high enough offer? Okay then. Antonia would crunch some numbers this weekend and
convince her brother Leo that even with paying a king's
ransom, they'd wind up with six or seven kingdoms in
the long run.

Anything to avoid thinking about the possibility of Charles saying something unkind about her.

She was about to tell Roth they could talk more about a possible new proposal—though only hinting at the final figure—when he returned to the matter at hand instead.

"Look, I really don't want to do this out here on the sidewalk," he said. "Is there someplace else we can talk?"

Antonia shook her head. "There is nothing to talk about where my fiancé is concerned. Whatever you think you heard him say about me, you were mistaken."

"Maybe you don't know him as well as you think you do."

"Oh, please. I know him backwards and forwards. He's perfectly suitable for me."

Roth's dark eyebrows shot up at that. "Suitable? That's not a word you usually hear people say about the person they're going to spend the rest of their lives with."

Okay, yes, that was a stupid word to have chosen. Why had her brain popped out that one? "He's more than suitable," she hastily amended. "I mean, yes, he travels a lot, but when he's here, he's completely devoted. And maybe his career has taken a hit in this economy, but it will rebound, and he'll be an excellent breadwinner. And maybe he sometimes doesn't say the right thing in social situations, but he's working on that…" She hurried to add when Roth opened his mouth to comment, "Bottom line? He's not perfect. None of us are. But he's perfect for me."

He studied her in silence for a moment, then said, "You know, what you just said about your fiancé sounded to me more like a CFO making a cost-benefit analysis."

Damn. How did he know that was exactly what Antonia had done before agreeing to marry Charles? She tried to tell herself it was no different than making a pros-and-cons list, which a lot of people did before deciding to get married. It was just good business. Um... she meant...it just made good sense.

"And *you're* beginning to sound a lot like my family," she replied before she could stop herself. Gia and Bella had told Antonia pretty much the same thing. Except Gia, marketing maven that she was, had said that what Antonia was running on Charles was a risk analysis. Ha ha ha.

Roth seemed very interested in that. "Your family doesn't like him, either?"

Either? Antonia echoed to herself. What did he mean by that? "They just don't know him the way I do," she said, echoing her own pep talk to herself from a few minutes ago.

"Or maybe *you* don't know him as well as you think you do," Roth said more softly. "If your family all have a problem with him, maybe you should take a better look at him yourself. In my experience, family never lets you down. They always know what's best for you."

Oh, easy for him to say. The Fortunes of Emerald Ridge had always been notoriously close. Not just Roth's branch of the family, but their distant Fortune cousins who lived here full-time were a famously tightknit bunch, too. Not that the Leonettis weren't close, but those Fortunes... Both sides were thick as thieves. As much as Antonia loved her family, she had to admit to a little twinge of envy that they still didn't seem as devoted as Roth and his siblings were.

She gave herself a mental shake, forcing her attention back to the matter at hand. "Look, Mr. Fortune—"

"Roth."

"Mr. Fortune," she reiterated more forcefully, "whatever you think you heard Charles say, it was—"

"He called you a cash cow."

This time it was Antonia's eyebrows that shot up to nearly her hairline. "There is no way Charles called me a cash cow."

"Okay, maybe he didn't use those exact words—"

"Of course he didn't. He would never do that."

"What he told his friend was that he was marrying you for your money. That once you and he were hitched, he'd be out of the red and into the black, thanks to the Leonetti money."

Antonia's mouth actually dropped open at that. "Okay, that just proves that you misunderstood what he said, because Charles has more money than he knows what to do with. His business is hugely successful. He's completed more than a dozen multimillion-dollar sales just since he and I started dating, and that's saying something in the current market."

Roth was shaking his head before Antonia even finished her first sentence. "Charles Cabot has completed zero deals since you and he started dating. If he told you otherwise, he was lying like a dog."

All Antonia could do now was stare at Roth in astonishment. Just what was he trying to do? He was the one who was lying, but why? How could he even know whether or not Charles was making sales?

All of those questions must have shown on her face, because he continued, "I spent the last couple of hours doing some digging. I know some people in Texas real estate. Word in the community is that Charles Cabot is completely washed-up. He doesn't have a nickel to his name. The fortune he built has been gone for years thanks to some terrible investments and his, um, his…" Here, Roth hesitated a telling moment before finishing, "His…overindulgences and lack of ethics. He's not even licensed to sell real estate in Texas anymore. His license got revoked because of some shady business practices a few years ago."

Antonia's initial reaction was to smack Roth Fortune upside the head and tell him to snap out of it. But all she could do was wonder why he would he lie about something she could prove wasn't true. Because he was definitely lying. He had to be.

"I don't believe you," she said simply.

"I wish I was wrong, Antonia, but I'm not."

A ripple of something strange and pleasant shimmied through her at the way he said her name. She didn't like the feeling at all. Not just because it had been generated by someone who was trying to blow up her life, but also because she had never felt anything like it when Charles said her name.

"Look, I don't know why you're doing this," she said, holding up a hand to silence him when Roth opened his mouth to speak again. "Maybe Charles and I don't have some big epic love, but we do have a lot of respect for each other. And we care about each other. I'm done with all that love and romance crap, anyway. Charles is a nice guy. He's funny. He's steady. I like him, and he likes me. And he'll be a good father to my daughter."

"And he said some not-so-nice things about your daughter, too."

Roth might as well have just slapped *her* this time, so swift and staggering was her reaction to his statement. "Like what?"

"He called her a snot-encrusted little rug rat."

Antonia blinked once. "I'm sorry, he called her what?"

"And a germ factory."

Now her fingers curled into fists. It was one thing for Roth to suggest Charles had ill will toward *her*. It was another thing entirely to go after her daughter. The mother bear inside her roared up to go on the attack— on Roth, not Charles, because she was absolutely certain now that he was lying. But she somehow managed to keep her voice, and herself, level.

"I think you need to leave," she said flatly.

Amazingly, Roth looked surprised by her offense. "But, An—"

"You may not call me by my first name. And you need to leave. Now."

"But—"

"I mean it, Mr. Fortune." She lifted her chin and took a step closer, enunciating emphatically every syllable so he heard every word she said. "I can't for the life of me imagine why you would approach me like this, when I'm about to be fitted for my *wedding gown*, and try to convince me my husband-to-be is a villain."

He hooked his hands on his hips and leaned in as heatedly as she had. "I'm doing it because your husband-to-be *is* a villain."

"Leave," she said. "Now. And never approach me again."

He shook his head. "Fine. If you want to marry a man who's going to bleed you dry and treat your child like a nuisance, and then take off with your hard-earned money when your five-year prenup expires, go ahead. Don't say I didn't warn you when you realize the truth."

Before she could utter another word, he spun on his heel and left. Antonia watched him go, still seething from what he'd said. How dare he come at her out of nowhere and say such horrible, hurtful things? Just who did Roth Fortune think he was?

And how did he know there was a five-year timeline on her prenuptial agreement with Charles?

She pushed the thought away. Lucky guess, or he'd also stuck his nose into other things that were none of his business over the last couple of hours. Antonia gripped the handle of the bridal shop door, yanked it open and stomped inside. Even the cool kiss of the air-conditioning and the sumptuous spectacle of gorgeous gowns and regalia did nothing to ease her anger. She inhaled deeply and counted to ten, until the edge of her fury had blunted some.

But it wasn't gone completely.

Try as she might, she couldn't quite shake the thoughts

intruding into her brain, notions that Roth Fortune had set free. When Carmen, the bridal shop manager, emerged from the back room to greet her, Antonia did her best to smile and focus on what should be a wonderful, soothing hour of trying on the most beautiful dress she'd ever own. It was hanging behind the counter waiting for her, its beads and sequins winking in the soft light of the shop as if trying to convince her that everything was going to be just fine. She told herself the dress was even more beautiful than she remembered. Instead, it suddenly looked gaudy and tawdry and cheap.

She looked at Carmen, who was reaching for the dress. "Carmen," she said, hoping her voice didn't sound nearly as cold as she suddenly felt. "Would it be a problem to reschedule my fitting? Something has come up."

Chapter Three

Roth pulled his midnight blue Porsche Carrera to a halt in front of the Leonetti mansion and told himself he still had time to turn around and go back home. He was probably the last person Antonia wanted to see right now. He wasn't even sure what had compelled him to drive over here in the first place. After their verbal exchange that afternoon, he was pretty certain she hated his guts. Even if everything he had told her was true.

Which, as it turned out, she'd discovered for herself—along with a lot of other unsavory things about the man she'd thought she was going to marry—shortly after telling Roth off. Emerald Ridge, Texas, might not exactly be a small town, but the grapevine here was every bit as busy. So it didn't surprise him at all that by dinnertime, pretty much everyone, including him, had heard about what had happened between her and Charles Cabot.

He told himself it was ridiculous for him to feel responsible for what she'd gone through today. Cabot was the one who was culpable for anything Antonia was feeling right now. Roth had just been the messenger. Unfortunately, he'd been a messenger who'd set into effect a chain reaction of terribleness that had taken mere hours to rocket through the entire town. How Antonia had gone to her fiancé's condo that afternoon when he thought she was being fitted for her wedding gown, and how she'd found him in bed with another woman. Who was essentially his secretary. And a decade younger than Antonia. If there had been any other way to make the whole thing a bigger cliché, Roth sure didn't know what it would be. He couldn't imagine how Antonia must be feeling right now—other than really, really bad.

Although it was well past the dinner hour now, the early August sun hadn't yet dipped below the horizon, instead washing everything around him in long rays of gold. The century-old Leonetti home was modeled after a Tuscan villa, its stone walls and terracotta roof fairly glowing against the amber of early sunset. Behind it, the vineyards rolled toward the horizon, adding a wide splash of green that helped give Emerald Ridge its name. And beyond them were the buildings of the business itself, likewise looking like something from a Mediterranean painting.

He told himself again that he should leave. Antonia was probably still processing what had happened, and she didn't need the interference of someone like him—an adversary now in both her professional *and* personal lives. But something inside him commanded he at least check on her in person. Even apologize to her for his part in what had transpired. Maybe she'd slam the door in his face after seeing him—and he wouldn't blame her—but at least he'd know he had tried. Mind made up, he reached for the Stetson in his passenger seat, exited his car, and approached the front door of the Leonetti home.

He hesitated only a moment before pushing the bell, then was surprised when Antonia herself was the one to answer the door. He didn't know what he'd expected— a housekeeper maybe, or even one of her siblings. Priscilla had filled him in earlier about how the whole family shared the house, save her brother, Leo, who kept to his own place now that he was engaged to Poppy Fortune, one of Roth's distant cousins. Antonia's sisters and mother and grandfather, though, three generations of Leonettis, still lived here, each of them claiming a different wing. As close as he was to his own siblings, Roth couldn't imagine sharing a house with the rest of the Fortunes year-round. Then again, if they'd lived in a house this big, they probably would have hardly ever seen each other.

Antonia didn't look great, which wasn't exactly surprising. The tidy tailored outfit she'd had on that afternoon had been replaced by a pair of—admittedly also tailored-looking—blue pinstriped pajama pants and an oversized white shirt. Her long, honey-brown hair was piled messily atop her head, a few errant strands dancing around her chin, and her tawny eyes were rimmed with red. She'd obviously been crying, but thankfully, there were no tears in sight now. When she saw him standing on the other side of the door, her eyes widened, and her lips parted softly.

"What are you doing here?" she said by way of a greeting. She didn't sound angry, though, just genuinely surprised. She seemed to realize the potential acrimony of the question, however, if not the tone, because she immediately continued, "I'm sorry. That came out badly."

She straightened to her full height. "Hello, Roth. What can I do for you?"

At least she was calling him by his name now and had dropped the absurd *Mr. Fortune.* Even the people he hired to work for him didn't call him that. He was Roth. Period. Unless he had to sign his name on some official document or something. Her question, though, was the same one she'd asked him that afternoon. The one he'd responded to by telling her that no, there was something he could do for *her.* At the time, he hadn't been thinking about how what he was going to do would be wrecking her life. He'd been thinking it would save it. What he hoped to be doing for her now was...

What? he asked himself. He still wasn't sure why he'd come here tonight.

He took off his Stetson and held it in both hands, a polite gesture that somehow also felt awkward. "I just wanted to apologize for this afternoon," he told her roughly.

At this, she looked puzzled. "Why would you feel like you need to apologize for anything?"

He lifted his shoulders and let them drop, then nervously shifted his Stetson from one hand to the other. "I kind of feel responsible for what happened this afternoon," he admitted. "After you and I...parted ways."

She nodded, looking very, very tired. "Yeah, well, what happened had nothing to do with you and everything to do with me and my terrible judgment regarding men. So you don't owe me an apology or anything else."

"If you need to vent, I could offer you a sympathetic ear."

She almost smiled at that. "Believe me, I've vented enough. Bella's and Gia's ears are probably still ringing. But at least neither of them said, 'I told you so.' Of course, for Bella, anyway, that might be because she went through something similar with her ex-husband while her own kids were preschoolers. Still, it was nice of my sisters to be sympathetic instead of judgmental, the way I fear many of the Emerald Ridge gossipmongers might be."

Roth nodded and wondered how to reply to that. He suddenly wished he had a magic wand he could wave to make everything better for this woman he barely knew and had never exactly been on good terms with. Why was that? he wondered. Maybe his breakup with Grace was still recent enough that he understood what it was like to be in Antonia's position. Then again, he'd been the one to initiate the split, and it hadn't been because she was cheating on him. In fact, as far as he knew, no woman had ever cheated on him. So, really, he had no idea what Antonia was going through right now. He still felt sympathetic, because he did know what it was like to be alone. And even if he told himself all the time that he didn't mind being alone—that he in fact preferred it—it still felt lousy sometimes.

Studying her up and down, he realized Antonia looked like the very definition of *lousy* right now. Not to mention the definition of *alone*. But nothing he could say or do would change that, as much as he wished it could.

"Well, then, I won't keep you…" Reluctantly, he put his hat back on, as if to physically illustrate his intention to leave her. Alone. Not that he wanted to do so.

But she didn't exactly seem like she wanted to invite him in, either. "I just wanted to be sure you were okay."

She surprised him when she opened the door a little wider. She seemed a little reluctant, though, when she asked him, "Would you like to come in? I was about to have a glass of wine, but something about drinking alone after the kind of day I've had makes me feel like even more of a cliché than I already do."

So he wasn't the only one who'd noticed that, huh?

"You're not a cliché," he assured her. He took off his hat again. "And I'd love to come in for a glass of vino."

She did smile at that, though it wasn't exactly a happy one. It was a start. When she took a few steps backward, Roth crossed the threshold into the house. The inside was as Italian villa-y as the outside, full of warm colors and natural accents. If he didn't know better, he would have felt like he had just flown into a quaint Tuscan village instead of having driven ten minutes outside Emerald Ridge, Texas. He'd learned a lot about the Leonetti business after buying his own vineyard—know your enemy and all that—how their grandfather Enzo had started it using old-world winemaking practices and designed the house to re-create the feel of the place he'd left behind when he migrated to the New World. The old man had obviously been as successful at evoking Italian charm as he had been at creating some of the most coveted wines in the world. No wonder the Leonettis were still notoriously family oriented. Their history and their house and the property surrounding it kind of ensured that they would be.

"This way," Antonia told him after closing the door

behind him. She tilted her head toward a sweeping stair-case that led to the second floor. Roth followed her as she climbed it, then turned left to head down a hall. "Gia and Bella and her kids live on the two floors of the east wing of the house, and my mother and grandfather live downstairs in this one," she told him as they made their way along. "Georgie and I have the upstairs on this side, so we all have plenty of room."

"It's a beautiful house," Roth said unnecessarily.

"Not much has changed since Papa first built the place."

She led him to the end of the hall, into what was clearly a combination sitting room and office space. Keeping with the old-world charm, the dark wood trim and bookshelves gleamed like satin, and the moss green walls were filled with paintings of what looked like the vineyard behind the house. A massive Persian rug spanned the hardwood floor under furniture that had been around a lot longer than Roth had. A wide iMac computer sat on a desk that looked like Christopher Co-lumbus himself might have used it, and the leather sofa and chairs were mellowed to a comfortable cognac color. He thought again about his own living space in Dallas, how sparse and monochromatic and, well, soulless it was. This room looked like a lot of living had gone on inside it. Like a lot of life still went on here. His place looked like no one had ever been there at all.

One section of the bookcases was honeycombed al-most floor to ceiling into a wine holder, generously filled with what he was going to go out on a limb and say were Leonetti vintages. Sure enough, the bottle Antonia withdrew from it was a Leonetti cabernet sauvignon, one of his favorites. Not that Roth was about to tell her how much he loved the Leonetti cabernets. Sure, they were on friendlier terms at the moment, but there was no reason she had to know how often he checked on the wines of her family to compare them to his own. Which competed nicely against theirs, if he did say so himself.

Anyway.

Antonia held up the bottle so that Roth could see the label more clearly. Wow, not only was it one of his favorite wines from Leonetti Vineyards, it was an incredible year for it. That bottle alone was worth a fortune. Antonia clearly intended to end what must have been one of the crappiest days of her life with a bang.

"This very wine was one of Jackie Kennedy Onassis's favorites," she said. "Well, not this particular year, but definitely this cabernet."

So Roth—and anyone else who loved wine—had heard.

"I was saving this bottle for my wedding day," she continued softly. "But since that's obviously not going to happen, ever, we can enjoy it tonight instead."

Well, if she insisted...

There was a rectangular white box with a small screen on a shelf next to the wine rack, and Antonia flicked a switch on it before fishing a corkscrew out of a basket beside it. The screen filled with a black-and-white shot of what looked like a baby crib with a baby sleeping soundly in the middle of it. The image was scored by the sound of a tinkling lullaby he didn't recognize coming from somewhere else in the room.

"Georgie's nursery is just across the hall," Antonia explained, noticing where his gaze had been drawn as she wound the corkscrew into the top of the bottle. "I want to be close enough to hear her if she starts to cry. She's had some nights lately where she hasn't been sleeping well for some reason."

Roth had seen Antonia pushing a stroller around town in the week since he and the rest of the Fortunes had been in Emerald Ridge, but he had no idea how old her daughter was. He hadn't even known until today whether she had a daughter or a son. From what he knew of babies and children—which was absolutely nothing— the kid in the stroller could have been anywhere from a month old to voting for the next governor.

"How old is your daughter?" he asked.

She tugged the cork from the bottle with a satisfying *pop*. "She'll be one year old next week," she told him with a smile. "I can hardly believe it." She continued talking as she pulled two wide-bowled wineglasses from a cabinet above the wine rack and began to pour. "She's gone from being this helpless, squirmy little Muppet wrapped in a blanket to a laughing, loving little bundle of wonder. She even talks now. With real words I can understand. *Mama* and *bear*, *hi* and *bye*, and *Bobo* and *Geega*."

"Bobo and Geega?" Roth asked, his lips quirking. Call him crazy, but those didn't sound like real words anyone could understand.

"That's what she calls Bella and Gia," Antonia said. "That makes them real words. Georgie is way ahead of other babies when it comes to language."

Roth nodded. "Sounds like."

"She calls Leo 'La.' So that's another word to add to the list."

If she said so. "Impressive," he told her.

"Damn right."

Antonia crossed the room and handed Roth his wine, then gestured toward the sitting area. He folded himself onto one side of the sofa, giving her plenty of room if she wanted the other side. Instead, she chose the chair across from him, something that allowed them to speak face-to-face more comfortably. She did seem to be in a better place than she was when she opened the front door to him. He would have liked to think it was because he just had a calming effect on people. Instead, he knew it was more likely that she'd just needed a distraction—any distraction—to make her feel better. But, hey, if his being here could make her world a better place, even if only for one evening, Roth would add it to the *Pro* column on his list of *Ways I've Affected the World*. There were times when he feared that column was way shorter than the *Con* side. He was just too busy for good deeds.

"I don't really know much about kids," he told her as she tucked one leg under the other in her chair. "No one in my immediate family has procreated yet. There are times when I wonder if any of us ever will."

"I hear you," she replied with a smile that was significantly less sad than the one she'd shown him before. "Georgie wasn't exactly planned. Don't get me wrong, I love her to pieces and can't imagine my life without her," she hurried to clarify. "But Silvio and I weren't planning on starting a family when it happened. We'd pretty much agreed to stay child-free."

"Silvio," Roth echoed. "That must be Georgie's father."

She nodded. "My ex-husband. We split up not long after I discovered I was pregnant. Two exes in two years." She lifted her wine as she muttered dolefully, "Here's to me. Queen of Bad Judgment."

Before she could sip her wine and make the toast legit, Roth told her, "You're not the Queen of Bad Judgment. Sounds to me like you're more the Queen of Optimism. Seeing the best in two men who didn't deserve a woman like you."

Yikes, had he really just said that out loud? Now that the thought was out of his mouth, it sounded like some cheesy come-on. He hoped she didn't take it the wrong way.

She stopped the glass short of her mouth. When she looked at him, however, she didn't seem to be thinking the comment was cheesy. Maybe it was conjecture on his part, but it seemed as if she didn't really consider herself an optimist at all. Finally, she compromised, replying, "Queen of Wishful Thinking," and took a small sip. After she swallowed, she lowered her glass again. "I was just so sure Charles would make a great husband and father. Then again, I was sure Silvio was my soulmate when I married him. Clearly, I need to think harder when it comes to men. Or, better yet, stop thinking about men at all."

"Yeah, well, for that," Roth said, "you really do deserve to be toasted. I should stop thinking about women myself. 'Cause when it comes to the opposite sex, my judgment isn't any better than yours."

He sealed the declaration with a lift of his own glass and healthy taste. Oh, yeah. That was good. Really good. The velvety wine went down like a sip of pure joy, warming his chest and belly on its way. He sipped again, savoring the flavor more leisurely. Damn. He needed to talk to his vintners about how they could re-create this experience for their clients.

Antonia chuckled, though whether she was reading his mind or responding to his comment, he honestly wasn't sure. Fortunately, she reassured him about the clairvoyance thing with her next comment. "Sounds like I'm not the only one who needs to commiserate about relationships. Recently stung yourself?"

Roth blew out a ragged sigh. "Kind of. Not that she was a soulmate or anything, but I did like her."

"What happened?"

No way was he going to sit here and complain about his own less-than-successful relationships when he'd come to focus on Antonia. So he only said, "We wanted different things for the future."

Antonia eyed him speculatively. "Why does that seem like another way to say she wanted to get married and start a family and you didn't?"

Was it that obvious? Instead of confirming her suspicions, though, he turned the tables back on her. "Like you said earlier about Charles. She wasn't the love of my life. And no way am I suited to be a family man."

She sounded a little mystified when she said, "I did tell you that about Charles, didn't I? I've never admitted that to anyone but myself. But no, he wasn't the love of my life. I thought he could be the something else of my life, though. Something else that was good and that would make me happy. Just not love. Romantic love doesn't exist."

"Well, you and I can definitely agree on that," Roth told her, sealing the sentiment with another taste of his wine. They were toasting a lot tonight. He'd had no idea he and Antonia Leonetti had so much in common.

"But now I've married for love and gotten engaged for practicality," she said, "and neither one of those things worked out. So where does that leave me? Other than alone for the rest of my life?"

"Hey, don't knock being alone. At least you're living with someone you can trust and tolerate."

She laughed lightly at that. "I guess." She lifted her glass again. "Here's to singlehood then."

He lifted his, too. "Now that I will definitely drink to."

Their gazes connected as they enjoyed another sip of their wine, then stayed connected as they both lowered their glasses.

"So you've never been married yourself?" Antonia asked.

He shook his head. "God, no. Not even close."

"Well, you don't have to sound so proud of the fact."

"I'm not proud. The truth is, I'm just like you. I don't believe in love. It's purely manufactured hooey that keeps a host of different industries in business." He grinned. "Where would Hollywood and Hallmark be without it? Or the flower and candy business? Hell, the whole wedding industry generates billions of dollars a year, and half of them don't even last."

"Spoken like a true venture capitalist."

He shrugged. "I'm not ashamed of what I do. I help create a lot of jobs for people. And I help a lot of folks turn their dreams into lucrative moneymakers."

"And now you're trying your hand at being a vintner."

He shook his head at that. "I'm not even going to pretend I'm a vintner. That takes way too much knowledge and skill and years of practice, and I don't have time for focusing on any of those things. I just always saw how much my dad loved being a hobbyist winemaker. Owning Fortune's Vintages kind of makes me feel closer to him, even though I'm not a vintner myself. I do have good people working for me in that regard," he added pointedly. "See? More jobs I'm creating."

She gazed at him thoughtfully. "At least you admit that winemaking isn't easy."

"Hell no," he agreed. "Which is why I'm not even going to try. I just want to enjoy the fruits of someone else's labor. Literally."

"Yeah, well, I'm not a vintner, either. That would be Bella in this family. I just crunch the numbers." She sipped her wine again. "And enjoy the fruits of someone else's labor."

"Touché." Now Roth was the one to laugh.

He stopped though, when a single soft cry came from the monitor on the other side of the room. Antonia looked over at the screen, too, her expression one of alarm, until Georgie cooed softly and went back to sleep. Then she relaxed. It struck Roth that it couldn't be easy to be a single mom to a baby that almost certainly commanded attention 24/7.

"So Georgie's father isn't a part of her life?"

Antonia shook her head. "Last I heard, he was back in Florence, where he grew up. Though he does move around a lot. He sends a check for Georgie every month that I deposit straight into her college fund, but that's it. I tried doing the FaceTime thing with him when Georgie was first born, so he could see how fast she was growing and changing. I was hoping that even though he and I had split, he would at least be a part of *her* life." She blew out a sigh. "But he would never spend more than ten minutes talking, and he only talked about himself. He never even asked how Georgie was doing and just kept interrupting whenever I tried to tell him about whatever milestones she had reached since my last call. Eventually he stopped showing up for the calls at all."

"I can't believe anyone would just turn their back on their own kid," Roth said, not quite able to contain his disgust.

"Well, he and I did decide before we married that we would never have kids, so I guess I shouldn't have been surprised."

"That doesn't excuse abandoning a child you're half responsible for and who needs all the love and support they can get while they're growing up."

Now Antonia smiled with genuine pleasure. "Listen to the hardened venture capitalist sounding like a big ol' softie."

In spite of the kindness of her comment, Roth rankled. That was two people in one day who'd implied that about him. "I'm not a softie."

"Okay. Whatever you say. You're hard as nails." Her smile, though, indicated she thought otherwise.

"I just think kids should be able to enjoy their childhood without bad things happening to them, that's all."

Her smile fell then, and she nodded. "I forgot you and your siblings lost your folks when you were kids. I'm sorry."

"It isn't just that," Roth said. "It's…" *What?* he asked himself. What the hell did he know about what kids needed to help them grow up into happy, healthy adults? Finally, he managed, "I just don't see how a person can turn their back on a child."

She nodded again, more soberly this time. "Georgie's birth totally changed my attitude about having a family," she confessed. "She's the best thing that ever happened to me. But having her didn't change Silvio's attitude at all. Having a baby, even part-time, would totally cramp his style trying to juggle a dozen different girlfriends. Some of whom he's had for more than a decade."

"But that means he was…" Roth stopped himself before saying the obvious. That her husband had had girlfriends—plural—the entire time he was married to her.

"Yeah. He was unfaithful. Like twice-or-three-times-weekly unfaithful the whole time we were together. Not that I knew that until after the split."

Ouch.

He was scraping his brain for something to say in response to that when the baby monitor erupted again. This time it wasn't a single cry, though. Nor was it followed by a softer coo. This time, it was an out-and-out screamfest. Antonia immediately set her wine on the coffee table and jumped up to race to the open door. Not sure what else to do, he followed her. She flung open the door to the room across the hall and hurried in. There was just enough pale blue light from the nightlight for him to see little Georgie standing inside the crib, gripping the side of it and howling, before Antonia scooped her up and into her arms. Where he would have thought that would soothe the baby and calm her down, she instead began to cry even harder. Antonia began to make a slow circuit around the room, bouncing Georgie softly as she murmured reassuring words into her ear. None of that seemed to work, either, though. The baby just kept crying.

"It's another nightmare, I think," Antonia said calmly over the din. "This has been happening a couple of times a week for the past month. She's teething again, too, and that doesn't help matters. I just don't know what to do except hold her and try to comfort her and let her cry it out."

A lot of parents probably did that when their babies cried, Roth thought. An inconsolable baby was probably nothing new to a mom or dad. Antonia was probably right that Georgie just needed to learn to comfort herself, knowing her mother was there to help.

Telling himself those things, however, did nothing to alleviate his own feelings of helplessness and distress. Georgie was so little, he couldn't help noting. She didn't have the language to tell anyone what was wrong. What if she was scared of something or in pain? She might be trying to articulate something really important that they had no way of understanding. It hit him hard, in some-place deep inside him, just how vulnerable and fearful a baby could be. It struck him even more profoundly how much he wanted to make Georgie feel better. But how was a guy like him, who knew nothing of children, supposed to soothe a troubled baby?

Antonia made another circuit around the nursery, stopping in front of Roth. "Maybe you could calm her down," she said over the baby's continued crying.

Panic shot through him. "What? Me? No. How am I supposed to console her? She doesn't even know who I am."

"I know, but she knows me better than anyone, and I'm not helping at all. Maybe having someone new hold-ing her will confuse her enough to make her stop cry-ing."

"But—"

Antonia ignored his suggestion and extended the wailing baby toward him. "Please?" she asked. "Just try?"

She sounded so scared, Roth couldn't find it inside himself to tell her no. Reluctantly, he held out both arms, hands turned toward the ceiling. He thought he would have trouble figuring out how to hold the baby. Antonia seemed to think he would have trouble with that, too, because she started to help him position his arms the right way. Surprisingly, though, he didn't have any dif-ficulty at all. Intuitively, he cradled Georgie in the crook of one arm while supporting her diaper-clad rump with his other hand. Also instinctive was how he started murmuring soft nonsense words to try to calm her down.

Then he was completely shocked when the baby stopped screaming and met his gaze with hers. For a moment, Georgie just stared at him, her dark curls spilling over her forehead, tears tumbling from her brown eyes, her little bottom lip quivering. Then, out of nowhere, she smiled at him. Even cooed at him. And then, she lifted a hand toward his face and…squeezed his nose.

He heard Antonia laugh softly beside him. Once he was over his surprise at the baby's gesture, he laughed lightly, too. That made Georgie chuckle along with them, then bring up her other hand to squeeze his nose with that one, as well.

"Does she think it's going to honk if she keeps doing it?" Roth asked, his smile widening.

"I have no idea," Antonia told him. "She's never done that to anyone before."

"Oh, so she's just trying to tell me I have a big nose, is that it?"

"You do not have a big nose," she assured him. "You have one of the most elegant noses I've ever seen."

Something in the way she said that made Roth turn now to look at Antonia. Although the only light in the room was a softly revolving nightlight throwing stars across the ceiling, he was pretty sure she was blushing.

His suspicions were confirmed when she stammered, "I mean…uh…it's just that…um…" She forced a smile that was probably supposed to be comical but instead looked a little panicked. But all she said was, "You don't have a big nose. Georgie just likes it for some reason."

As if to drive that point home, the baby squeezed his nose again. Unable to help himself, Roth made a soft honking sound when she did, and the baby fell into a fit of giggles. He couldn't help but chuckle too. He'd never been this close to a baby before and certainly never heard one laugh. Georgie's was infectious. There was a purity and innocence about it he just couldn't ignore. He couldn't remember the last time he'd found something as funny about anything that Georgie found about his honking nose.

"You're really good with her," Antonia said softly.

"I've only been holding her for a minute," he pointed out. "And I'm a stranger. Like you said, I'm just a distraction to whatever was bothering her."

There it was again. Him being a distraction. Was that all he'd ever be to the Leonetti women? And why did he suddenly want to be more than that? When he looked at Antonia again, she was gazing at him in a way that made something in the pit of his belly spark to life, sending a sizzle of heat through his entire body. Including places that had no business feeling sizzle for Antonia Leonetti.

He extended Georgie back toward her mother with a hastily proffered, "Here. I'm sure she'd rather have her mother."

But instead of going willingly to Antonia, Georgie tried to cuddle against Roth again. Even when she was back in her mother's arms, she reached for him.

"I should probably get going," he said without thinking. "Let you get her back to sleep."

"You don't have to rush," Antonia objected. "Now

that she's stopped crying—however you managed that— she'll probably nod right off again."

Leaving him and Antonia to talk some more. Alone. About things he sure as hell had never talked about with women on a first date. Not that this was a date, he hastily reminded himself. He'd just come over to make sure Antonia was okay. And now that he knew she was, as was her daughter, there was no good reason he could think of to hang around at this point. But there were a million good reasons he could think of to leave. Starting with the one about oversharing more of himself in a matter of minutes with Antonia than he'd done with a dozen other women after months of seeing them.

"It's getting late," he said, even though it still wasn't full dark outside. "I should let you and Georgie get on with your evening."

"But—"

"Let me know if I can do anything to help you out," he added as he began to back toward the nursery door. "Aside from selling you Fortune's Vintages, I mean," he clarified, in case she tried to bring that up again. Which she most likely wouldn't, since she had a baby to get back to sleep.

But hey, that just went to show how different he and Antonia were, he told himself triumphantly. He was focused on business in that moment, when she was focused on family. Had he been thinking earlier that the two of them had a lot in common? Pshaw. They were as far apart as two people could be. And if he had an ounce of sense left, he'd get out of there right now and put them at an even greater distance.

He had reached the nursery door by now and was about to bolt down the hall and out of the house before he got himself into more trouble. Then he remembered his favorite Stetson was still in the other room and hesitated. His biggest mistake yet.

Because as Antonia and Georgie continued to look at him—both of them still smiling in a way Roth didn't like one bit—Antonia announced, "Hey, we're having a party for Georgie's first birthday on Thursday. Why don't you come? I think Georgie likes you."

Roth told himself to politely decline. He was about to, but then she said something to make that very difficult.

"There will be cake and ice cream."

Damn. "What kind of cake?" he asked.

"Chocolate with white icing."

His absolute favorite. But he could still resist. As long as she didn't tell him the ice cream was chocolate chip.

"And chocolate chip ice cream," she added.

He told himself he could still resist. But then, out of nowhere, he heard himself say, "That sounds like fun. Thanks for inviting me. I'd love to come."

"Great," Antonia said.

"Gah," Georgie chimed in with a laugh.

Antonia looked at her daughter, stunned, then back at Roth. "Did you hear that? She said, 'great,' too! Another new word! She totally wants you to come."

Roth couldn't help smiling at that. New moms sure could be delusional when it came to baby milestones. Not that he minded. And truth be told, Georgie had kind of sounded like she was saying *great*.

"Great," he threw in, too.

"It's at twelve noon," Antonia said. "The theme is My First Rodeo. Like, you know, the party actually *is* her first rodeo."

Roth grinned. "Clever."

"Anyway, be there or be square, cowboy. Be here, I mean," she hastily corrected herself. "We're having it here at the house. Outside in the backyard. Cake and ice cream on us."

"Count me in," he said.

"Great," Antonia replied.

"Gah," Georgie chimed in.

He lifted a hand in farewell to them both, crossed the hall to collect his hat, then found his way back downstairs to the front door. Outside, the sky was smudged with the purples and pinks of twilight, and the sun had dipped behind the trees. A voice inside Roth's head told him he should never have agreed to go to a party—a child's birthday party, no less—where Antonia Leonetti would be around. They were still business rivals. Plus, she was fresh off a broken romance that had ended very badly for her. And on top of all that, she was a single mom, and he didn't know the first thing about kids. There was nothing—absolutely nothing—that should make him want to see her again.

And he didn't want to see her again, he reassured himself right back. Not the way the voice inside him seemed to be suggesting. It was a kid's birthday party, for crying out loud. Not exactly the atmosphere for starting anything anyway. Not that he wanted to start something with Antonia Leonetti. Or that there was even anything to start. He just wanted to be sure she and

Georgie were both okay. Plus, he liked rodeos. And cake and ice cream. And parties, for that matter.

The fact that he was beginning to kind of like Antonia, too, was completely beside the point.

Chapter Four

Antonia was exhausted when she went down to breakfast the morning after Roth's surprise visit to the house. Georgie had become distraught again after he left, and although she hadn't fallen into fits of inconsolable crying as had been the case on so many nights, she'd fought hard against going back to sleep. Antonia had ended up bringing the baby into her own room and settling her into the bassinet beside the bed that she hadn't used for months. Georgie had still fretted and babbled enough to keep them both up most of the night, though she finally fell into a deep slumber just before dawn.

Antonia herself had lain awake wide-eyed, replaying every word she and Roth had exchanged during their conversation the evening before. She still couldn't believe she had opened up so much to someone she barely knew. To someone who was her *professional enemy.* She hadn't talked that much about her marriage to anyone outside her family before, even people she'd known for years. And certainly never to a business rival. In case that part needed hammering home. Which it obviously did, because she'd done just that last night. Why had she found it so easy to confide in Roth?

Fatigue, she told herself. Sleep deprivation could wreak havoc on a person's mental state in even the best of circumstances, let alone after an extremely emotional day like she'd had. Thank goodness Georgie's nanny, Kayla, had agreed to come in on a Sunday in addition to the three days a week she worked when Antonia went into the office. *Kayha*, as Georgie called her, was upstairs at that very moment, making sure the baby didn't sleep in so much that her entire nightly sleep cycle got interrupted. Now Antonia would be able to spend the day focusing on…

What was it she was supposed to be focusing on today? Oh, right. All the work she'd been neglecting while she'd been planning a wedding that wasn't going to take place now. Not some handsome guy in a Stetson who had cradled her daughter with such gentleness and reassurance the night before. What Antonia really needed most at the moment was coffee. What she needed second most was a swift kick in the pants.

What had she been thinking inviting Roth Fortune into her home the evening before? Immediately, she answered her own question: she hadn't been thinking at all. She'd been so surprised to find him on her doorstep that all thoughts had dried up in her head. Then again, what had actually made her lose her mind was how good he'd looked standing there. Maybe the two of them were at odds professionally, but personally, she didn't think she'd ever seen a more handsome man. Bathed in the pale gold of the setting sun, literally standing there hat in hand, he'd looked like a Western movie antihero. The gunslinger with a heart of gold checking up on the rancher's widow who was trying to fight off the evil cattlemen encroaching on her land. Not that Antonia was a rancher's widow. Or that there were any evil cattlemen in Emerald Ridge, encroaching or otherwise. But regardless, Roth had still looked like an antihero. An irresistible one at that. And she really needed a hero.

Oh, yeah. She was definitely not getting enough sleep if she had Shrek's Fairy Godmother singing about needing a hero stuck in her head. Even if—there was no sense in her denying it—Roth Fortune had made her heart race like some kind of pop song hero. She was only human, after all. Whose heart wouldn't race when they were standing within inches of those Caribbean blue eyes and chiseled cheekbones and the kind of mouth that made a woman want to wreak mayhem? And shoulders that had seemed as broad as the porch behind him. Not to mention a solid torso that narrowed to a waist just begging for her arms to reach out and circle it, then pull him close and then—

Coffee, Antonia told herself again, interrupting thoughts that needed interrupting before they went any further. She needed coffee. Lots of it. Stat.

"Good morning, late riser," Gia sang out when Antonia entered the dining room.

Both of her sisters were seated at the table, Bella dressed in her Sunday-morning marketing maven outfit of linen trousers and tunic, and vintner Gia in her usual jeans and T-shirt. They each had their dark hair drawn back, but where Gia wore a simple ponytail, Bella wore a tidy bun. Absently, Antonia ran a hand over the pajamas she was still wearing and did her best to push away the loose strands of hair she could feel dancing around her face, in spite of having loosely braided it before going to bed. It wasn't unusual for her to feel less put together than her sisters. But at the moment, she was particularly aware of it.

"It is morning," she conceded to Gia's greeting. "Whether or not it's good depends on if there's any coffee left."

"I just brewed a fresh pot," Bella told her.

"Then yes. It is a good morning."

She was making her way to the kitchen—and sending silent thanks to her big sister for having had the foresight to know how badly she would need a whole pot all to herself—before she even finished speaking. She poured a cup, added her usual sugar and half-and-half, then grabbed an apple and a banana from a basket on the counter. When she returned to the dining room, she folded herself into a chair opposite Gia and immediately to Bella's right. One of them had placed a box of pastries from Emerald Ridge bakery on the table, and a peek inside told Antonia her sisters had been kind enough to leave two orange scones, her favorite, untouched amid the crumbs. Her stomach rumbled at the sight and scent.

Setting aside the fruit she'd brought with her, she grabbed a scone instead. Then—what the hell, she only lived once—she grabbed the other one, too. Hey, she had a big day ahead of her, facing down town gossips and trying not to think about Roth Fortune and his incredible shoulders and waist and eyes and mouth and… Um, anyway, she was going to need all the energy she could get.

"So whose *very* nice car was that that I saw parked out front when I got home from dinner with a potential client last night?" Bella asked. Looking right at Antonia. Dammit. So much for not thinking about Roth Fortune.

Even so, "Why are you asking me?" Antonia said in an effort to sidestep the question without lying. Her sisters had always been able to tell when she was lying.

Like right now, for instance, even though she wasn't exactly fibbing. Bella and Gia exchanged one of those eye-rolling glances that stopped just short of actual eye-rolling.

"Because *I* was out with the kids last night," Gia said. "Which I told Bella when she asked me about it. Mom and Papa are always pretty much turned in for the night by sundown, so it must have been someone you know."

The reason Papa, their grandfather, was always in for the night before nightfall was because he was taking life easier these days after a battle with liver cancer that had nearly taken him from all of them last spring. Although Enzo was in full remission now and back to his spirited, lovable, full-of-advice-about-love-and-life self, his eighty-two-year-old body was moving a bit more slowly these days. And their mother, Martina, had lived a pretty quiet life all around since their father's death ten years ago. Their brother, Leo, came and went at the house, and people still dropped by looking for him sometimes, but he kept to his own place now that he and his fiancée, Poppy, were starting their life together with baby Joey.

Not that Leo had ever spent much time at the mansion, anyway, in spite of being CEO of the family business. He was only CEO because their grandfather and father both had been old-school about how it took a Y chromosome to run a business. This in spite of the fact that at least two, and maybe all three, of their grand-daughters/daughters had been way more equipped, and even eager, to take over the vineyard than Leo, and... and...

And where was she? Oh, right. She'd been trying to evade her sisters' question about whose car had been parked out front the evening before. "I thought Mom had her book club last night," she said, still being eva-sive. "And Papa might have a new friend, who knows?"

"Mom's book club was last week," Gia said.

"And although Papa makes a new friend pretty much every day," Bella added, "few of them still drive after the sun goes down. Especially a stick shift. So whose car was it, Antonia?"

Antonia bit back an exasperated sound. She really didn't want to have this conversation on not even half a cup of coffee. But she knew better than to keep sidestep-ping her sisters. They wouldn't let this go until they got an answer. A real answer. Not a made up one like *Oh, that was Santa Claus stopping by to make sure Georgie was still on the Nice list.*

She sighed. "It was Roth Fortune's."

Antonia might as well have just told her sisters it was a clown car that had erupted with a whole circus for Georgie's enjoyment, so clear was their surprise.

"Roth Fortune came here?" Gia asked with much in-terest. "Why? Is he having second thoughts about selling Fortune's Vintages? Did you send him a new proposal no one told me about?"

Bella looked just as invested. "I would so love to get my hands on some of those grapes. I don't know what his vintners are doing over there, but wow, has that vineyard come a long way since he bought it."

Antonia shook her head. "There has been no new proposal," she assured them before they could get too far into their financial and agricultural planning. "And even if there had been, I'm reasonably certain he still has no intention of selling to us. He just wanted to apologize to me."

Now her sisters looked confused.

"For what?" Gia asked.

"Not selling us Fortune's Vintages?" Bella added hopefully.

"No, for what happened with Charles yesterday."

"Why would Roth Fortune apologize," Gia said, "for something that that creepy, slimy, disgusting…"

"Horrible, gross, obnoxious…" Bella threw in.

"Nasty, cretinous, sleazy…"

"Greedy, malignant, icky…"

"You guys have been hitting the thesaurus pretty hard for Charles," Antonia said. Not that she hadn't uttered all those words to herself—and then some—over the course of yesterday and last night.

"Anyway, why would Roth apologize for what that scumbag Charles did?" Bella asked.

"Because he was the one who put the series of unfortunate events into motion," Antonia told them.

She quickly explained what she had left out in her ranting to them yesterday, about how it had been Roth who alerted her to Charles's intentions after overhearing a conversation earlier that morning, and about how he'd told her he himself had looked into Charles's finances and found them to be a tad lacking. About how she hadn't believed Roth at first, but the suggestion that her fiancé wasn't on the up-and-up had settled just deeply enough into her brain to send her to his condo to ask him about it. She didn't have to add the part about finding her fiancé in bed with his fresh-out-of-business-school secretary after using her key to his place to let herself in. That last part they already knew, along with every-one else in Emerald Ridge by now.

It was strange, though, how, thinking and talking about it again this morning, Antonia didn't feel nearly as teary or sad as she had yesterday. Today, she mostly felt angry. Angry at Charles for being so horrible and angry at herself for falling for him in the first place. But as furious as she was about being made a fool by Charles, she was even more livid for how cavalierly he had been toward her daughter. Their prenup had speci-fied that neither of them would be entitled to any re-muneration—or anything else—if the marriage ended earlier than their five-year anniversary. In that amount of time, Georgie would have bonded with Charles in a way that would have made him a virtual father to her. She would have been devastated once he turned his back on both of them. To be abandoned by not one but two fathers, at such a young age… There wasn't enough therapy in the world to heal that.

Then again, Antonia had been abandoned twice now herself. But it was one thing for Charles to have been so heartless to an adult like her. It took an even more malevolent monster to hurt a child. She'd get over Charles Cabot. Eventually. However, Georgie might never have fully recovered had she grown to love him like a father.

Of course, considering how mad Antonia was this morning, she seemed to be getting over Charles already.

"Wow, you owe Roth Fortune a huge debt," Gia said while Antonia was mulling that over.

Gia nodded. "I'll say. If he hadn't overheard what he had and then told you about it, you would have gone through with the wedding and ended up in an even worse situation."

It stunned Antonia to hear her sisters speak of Roth Fortune in such glowing terms after years of all of them badmouthing him. A mere twenty-four hours ago, all of the Leonettis had considered him nothing but a pain in the butt for being so contrary about selling the vineyard they'd wanted for so long and that was eating into their profits with every passing year. Now, suddenly, they owed him a huge debt of gratitude? Not that Antonia wasn't grateful to him for alerting her to the kind of man Charles was. But she'd hardly say she owed him her eternal gratitude. When he told her what he overheard, he'd just been being a decent person, that was all. Anyone in the same position would have alerted her the same way.

Then again, if Charles had been bragging to one person—in public, no less—about how he planned to take advantage of Antonia, he may very well have told others, too. And no one else—including the guy he'd been having lunch with yesterday, who Antonia had realized after the fact was someone Charles had introduced her to on more than one occasion—had said a word to her about what he was planning to do or how he really felt about her and her daughter.

"We all owe Roth Fortune a debt," Gia continued, surprising Antonia even more. "He could have really done a number on the Leonetti family finances after he dumped you."

Bella's eyes went wide again. "Holy moly, I never thought about that. We need to be nicer to the guy in the future."

Now Antonia was the one to look at her sisters in disbelief. "Are you guys kidding me? He's the competition!"

"Right," Gia said, nodding at the reminder.

"True," Bella concurred.

Though neither of them sounded very competitive in their concessions.

Antonia tried again. "We can't let this one episode of decency on his part change our intentions toward him. We still need to keep an eye on Fortune's Vintages, and we still need to see him as the opposition. He's our biggest local business rival, after all. Which means that when it comes to the Leonetti Vineyards bottom line, the man is dangerous."

Her sisters nodded their silent agreement, yet still didn't look particularly convinced.

Antonia lifted her cup for another sip of coffee. "Anyway, he's coming to Georgie's birthday party next week."

Okay, that finally did get a more expressive reaction.

"Wait. You invited him to Georgie's birthday party

Thursday?" Gia asked. "I thought he was our enemy and dangerous to our bottom line."

"Yeah, that doesn't sound very business rival-y to me," Bella agreed.

"Well, it was the least I could do," Antonia pointed out, "what with him saving me—and my entire family—from financial chaos. Besides, he was really good with Georgie last night."

"Hang on. You actually introduced him to Georgie?" Bella asked.

"You didn't even introduce Charles to Georgie until you guys had been dating for months," Gia added.

Antonia realized her mistake in that revelation. She'd always been a tigress about protecting her daughter from the outside world. That Roth had just waltzed right in and become a part of things within minutes of his arrival at the house...

Some tigress she'd turned out to be. Even if Roth had been like a magic charm where her daughter was concerned.

"Um, yeah," she admitted to her sisters. "But only because Georgie was crying again, and I couldn't get her calmed down. Roth was able to settle her the minute he held her."

Her sisters exchanged another, this time very knowing, look, then turned their attention back to Antonia. Then they both smiled. In a way that made her want to squirm in her seat.

Especially when Bella cooed, "And he does have some pretty dreamy blue eyes, doesn't he?"

Antonia dropped her gaze to her coffee. Hmm. She

hadn't added enough half-and-half. "I never said any-thing about his dreamy blue…ah, I mean… I never said anything about his eyes."

"No, but you were thinking it."

"He's like the epitome of tall, dark and handsome," Gia said with a sigh.

"Yes, he is," Bella concurred.

"I bet Roth Fortune and his dreamy eyes turn a lot of heads," Gia added.

"Stop it," Antonia scolded her sisters. Even though she herself had used the words *tall*, *dark* and *handsome*, not to mention *dreamy eyes*, herself when thinking about Roth the day before. "My invitation to the man had noth-ing to do with any of that. I only invited him as my way of saying thank you for his help with Georgie, and he's only coming because he likes cake and ice cream."

"Of course," Gia said, still smiling. "I'm positive that's the only reason you invited him and the only rea-son he accepted the invitation."

"It is," Antonia insisted. "I mean, he does. Like cake and ice cream, I mean. He told me so himself."

Even to her own ears, the explanation seemed lame. Just why had Roth agreed to come to Georgie's birthday party? she wondered. More to the point, why had she invited him? And why oh why was she kind of looking forward to having him come?

She looked at her sisters. Gia and Bella looked back at her. They were still smiling. What was weird was that, on some level, somewhere deep inside her, Antonia realized she was smiling, too. And having just come off the kind of day she'd had the day before, she couldn't for the life of her figure out why that would be.

Chapter Five

Tuesday evening found Roth running late for dinner with the rest of his family at the main house on the Fortune compound. It had been a hell of a day. Even though he'd been pretty confident it wouldn't be an issue for him to work remotely here in Emerald Ridge for the duration of August, it was starting to become a problem. He'd actually had to drive back to Dallas late yesterday morning to meet with an overly anxious client about one of her investments, one he'd assured her was going to quadruple her money, provided she just let it ride. It had taken him half a day to talk the woman down, and it had been so late by the time they finished their meeting that Roth had decided to just sleep at his place instead of returning to Emerald Ridge.

Weirdly, though, the minute he walked through the door to his high-rise condo last night, he hadn't felt like he'd come home at all. The place had seemed more foreign to him than a hotel room would have felt. It had just been so…cold. So lacking in color. Hell, so lacking in *life*. Too beige, too quiet, too empty. Even the bright lights of Dallas beyond the windows hadn't helped. They'd only hammered home to him how many people there were out there, living the way he did—surrounded by others looking out at the world beyond the window instead of being out there living in it. Even after turning on some Sturgill Simpson to chase away the silence and flipping on the gas fireplace to give the living room some phony warmth, Roth had felt surrounded by, well, nothing.

Maybe he'd get a dog after he and his family returned home from Emerald Ridge, he thought as he made the walk to the main house now. Someone to meet him at the door at the end of a long day, who he could take out for a run in a good-sized park and—

Except there weren't many good-sized parks in downtown Dallas. Or, you know, any good-sized parks. He and his alleged dog would mostly run on concrete. And the poor animal would have to be left alone all day while Roth worked, which wasn't a great way to be...

Okay, so maybe he was no more fit to be a dog owner than he was to be a family man. He shook off the unrest that had been with him since leaving his sterile condo this morning and reminded himself he was back in Emerald Ridge now, surrounded by family and all the green space he could ever want. Little by little, his body relaxed and the clouds in his head scattered. And as the main house appeared in the distance ahead of him, he kind of felt like, yeah, okay, *now* he was going home. This place was certainly closer to being a home than anything he'd had as an adult.

One of the reasons his parents had bought the property before he and his siblings were born was because there was enough acreage for them to build guest houses for the kids they planned to have at some point. Kids who could—and *would*, the elder Fortunes were certain—use the houses as adults. Mark and Marlene had told their children every summer when they were vacationing in Emerald Ridge about how they'd looked at the riverfront property as newlyweds and imagined a whole passel of children—and, later, grandchildren—laughing and running with water balloons in the bright summer sun, or cannonballing into the sparkling waters of the river at the end of the pier, or picnicking on the beach in their damp swimsuits at sunset as fireflies danced around them. Then, as each of their children had been born, they'd had an additional, smaller mini-mansion built to complement the main house, knowing that, when the two of them were old and gray, they could host their whole, big, constantly growing family for summers and holidays well into their golden years.

Roth wished more than anything that that was exactly how his parents' lives had played out. He didn't even mind that they probably would have been super disappointed that none of their children had started families by now. Had they been alive today, Mark and Marlene would have been giving him and his siblings an earful every time they visited about how the houses weren't being put to use the way they had been intended, and when were he, Harris, Zara and Priscilla going to get married and start families of their own?

He smiled as he climbed the front steps to the main house. Even after two decades, he could still hear his mother's voice clear as day, and she would for sure be asking him precisely those questions.

Sorry, Mom, he replied to her silently, sending an apologetic look skyward. *It's not as easy these days as it was for you and Dad*. His parents had lucked out in finding each other in the big wide world when they were both young. And Roth didn't care what anyone said, times pre-internet had been a lot simpler. The world was even bigger and wider now, and relationships were way more complicated. Hell, none of the four Fortune kids had come close to getting married or starting a family. Neither had his cousin Kelsey—or Sander, for that matter, having been single since his daughter was a baby. That just went to show how different things were now.

Phooey, he could hear his dad's voice say in retort, likewise clear as day. *You meet a nice girl, you fall in love, you settle down. Worked for your mom and me.*

Roth sighed as he turned the knob to enter the house. Man, he wished he could have just one day to spend with his parents again. There was so much he wanted to tell them about all four of their children. Not just about how well he'd done himself with Fortune Capital, but how well the rest of their kids had turned out. How Harris had survived the awkward puberty he was going through when they last saw him, how he was outpacing even Roth with his import/export business, and how he had a stronger moral compass and more integrity than any human being Roth had ever met. And how Zara, who'd always found it so hard to let anyone get too close, was now a successful matchmaker who gave her heart to every client and wanted to see everyone in the world live happily ever after. And last but certainly not least, how Priscilla had become such a social butterfly, kind and soft-hearted toward, oh, everyone. His parents would have been proud of all of them if they could see them now.

Okay, except for the part about how none of them had produced grandchildren for them. But there was still time for that. For his siblings, anyway, since Roth couldn't see himself ever becoming a father. Kind of hard to do when you weren't the kind of person to settle down with anyone.

For some reason, that made him think about Antonia Leonetti. Which was another reason he was running late for dinner. Even after such an exhausting day in Dallas yesterday, he'd barely slept a wink last night. His brain had been too busy replaying the Saturday evening before at the Leonetti home. It had just been such a strange night.

What he heard when he opened the front door to the main house and walked through it, though, was even stranger. Voices calling out from upstairs to downstairs and what sounded like furniture being dragged from one side of a room to another on both floors. Had he arrived so late that he'd missed dinner? He glanced at his watch. Nope. It was only fifteen minutes past the time he'd been told to show up. And he could smell whatever Sander was making tonight—his famous Tex-Mex black bean chili, judging by the luscious aroma—coming from the kitchen.

"Did you find anything yet?" he heard his uncle call from that direction.

"Nothing!" his cousin Kelsey replied to her father from the opposite direction. "I'm telling you, whatever it is isn't in the main house! We've looked everywhere!"

She was referring to the long-lost family surprise his parents had hidden somewhere on the property, Roth deduced. He and the rest of the Fortunes had been searching for it since their arrival, whenever any of them had a free moment. But just like had been the case in every previous summer that they'd tried, there was no trace of it.

So far, he told himself. The six of them had made a pact over dinner that night in Dallas before leaving for Emerald Ridge that *this* year, even if they had to hire an army of bloodhounds or the salvaging team that had located the *Titanic*, they were going to find it.

Kelsey entered the living room from the dining room beyond it, brushing her hands together as if trying to rid them of dust. At twenty-five, she was the baby of the family, almost as much a sibling as Roth's actual siblings were. Certainly they all loved her like a sister. Her long auburn hair spilled over one shoulder, and her oversized shirt and jeans were streaked with what looked like the gritty remnants of a deep dive into a long-neglected closet.

"It has to be in one of the guesthouses!" she called out over her shoulder. "It just isn't—" She halted when she saw Roth standing in the foyer and smiled. "Well, hello there, stranger. Long time, no see. Missed you at breakfast. And lunch. And dinner last night. Where've you been?"

They'd all agreed that they would share as many dinners here at the house as they could while they were in Emerald Ridge and trade off cooking and cleaning duties. Or dinner buying in the case of those who had neither the knowledge nor the inclination to cook—like Roth. His turn was still two nights away, which was why he hadn't been overly concerned about spending the night last night in Dallas. Last time he'd hosted, he'd treated the family to a very nice dinner at Lone Star Selects steakhouse. It had set him back a pretty penny, though, so next time he was either going to have to go with pizza from Donatello's or a bag full of sandwich fixings.

It wasn't that he didn't know how to cook. Their mother had made sure all of them knew their way around a kitchen when they were growing up, and as the oldest, he'd had more training than any of them. Truth be told, his own beef fajita chili was even better than Sander's black bean, if he did say so himself. But who had time for cooking a meal every day? Or even once a week, as far as he was concerned. He never did that in Dallas. Much easier to pay someone else to do it, then take it home to eat. Alone.

He bit back an exasperated growl and asked his brain to go easy on all the alone stuff it seemed to be focusing on lately. Then he lifted a hand with a single wave of greeting to his cousin.

"Hello yourself," he said. "I had to drive back to Dallas for a business meeting yesterday and ended up spending the night. Then I took advantage of being there to tend to some more business this morning. But I think I should be good for the rest of the month." He hoped so, anyway. He liked being here in Emerald Ridge.

Which was an odd thing to realize, because he hadn't exactly been looking forward to even the long weekend the family had originally planned to spend here, and he'd nearly panicked when they all decided to stay until at least the end of the month, with the hope that Linc's murder would be solved by then. Roth had been itching to get back to Dallas the minute he left its city limits a week and a half ago. However, since coming to Emerald Ridge and spending more time with his family than he had in years, and since running into so many old friends—and kind of making new ones in people like...oh, he didn't know... Antonia Leonetti—his perspective was changing.

"Excellent," Kelsey said. "'Cause we can really use your help looking for the great, big whatever it is your parents stashed here twenty years ago. Not that it's big or great, necessarily, because if it was, we probably would have found it by now. But it could be. Who knows?"

None of them, that was for sure. Not even Sander, who was their father's younger brother and the only one of them who had been an adult—barely—when Mark and Marlene died. Roth's parents had been surprisingly tight-lipped about the whole thing, in spite of their obvious excitement. He remembered how both of them had smiled, though, whenever they mentioned the fun the kids were going to have looking for it, as if what they'd hidden was the greatest treasure their children would ever know.

What that treasure might be, though, he couldn't imagine. Even as kids, they'd had everything they ever wanted and the best family in the world, which was the greatest gift anyone could ask for. Mark and Marlene Fortune had spared no expense when it came to making their children happy. Every Christmas, Santa had left them just about everything they wrote on their lists. Their Easter baskets had runneth over. Even the Tooth Fairy had left them more than their friends and class-mates ever received. When they were kids, Roth and his siblings had figured it was just because they were at the very top of every Good Boys and Girls list that was out there.

As adults, of course, they knew it had just been one more way their parents had showed them how much they loved them. Yes, the Fortunes were rich. He could say that matter-of-factly because it was the truth. But his parents had worked hard to earn and keep their wealth, and their philanthropy had been as large as their hearts. They'd passed both their work ethic and their altruism on to their children. Whatever this wonderful surprise was, once they found it—*if* they found it—Roth was sure it would be as beautiful as his parents had been.

"It's not in my house," he told his cousin in response to her earlier statement. "I've looked everywhere."

Okay, almost everywhere, he amended to himself. He supposed it was possible there was a loose floorboard or hidden hidey-hole he didn't know about. And yeah, maybe he'd only turned his own bedroom and bathroom upside down, not the other three bedrooms or the sec-ond and third baths. And there were some kitchen cabi-nets he hadn't looked too deeply into. Maybe a couple of closets, too. And the patio. He hadn't looked that hard out there, either.

All right, fine. He hadn't looked that hard anywhere

in his house. He was still reasonably certain it wasn't there.

Kelsey grinned as if reading his mind. "We'll all come over and have a look at your place later this week."

"Better check everyone else's house, too," Roth told her.

"Oh, we for sure will."

Sander entered from the other side of the room, looking as disheveled as his daughter. Although he was forty-four, he didn't look much older than Roth. The two of them could have passed for brothers, really, though the physical resemblance was slight. Sander's overlong hair was blond instead of dark, peppered with a hint of silver, and he liked to go more than a few days without shaving most of the time where Roth took as much care with his daily regimen as he did with his wardrobe. His clients were generally conservative people who wanted someone as clean-cut as they were themselves handling their investments. The rugged stubble looked good on Sander, though, making him seem more like cowboy than an architect of some of the most beautiful ranches in the state. When Roth was a kid, he'd thought his uncle actually *was* a cowboy, so confident was he around horses and so sure was his swagger. He'd been floored when his father explained to him that no, Sander did not punch cows, he punched a time clock, just like normal people.

Even now, he still kind of looked like a cowboy to Roth. There was something about the glint in his hazel eyes and the howdy-do grin curling his mouth that just reeked of the Wild West.

"It might not be in any of the guesthouses," Sander

said now. "Could be in the boathouse. Or, hell, one of the boats for that matter."

If Mark Fortune had had his way, Roth knew, he would have collected boats. The old Bristol sailboat and Chris-Craft cruiser housed in the Fortunes' boathouse had been his father's pride and joy, second only to his family when it came to bringing him happiness. Sander and Roth and Harris had kept both vessels in tiptop shape since his death, having them serviced regularly, and they all still took both boats out on the river whenever they were in Emerald Ridge. They were decent-sized boats, especially the Bristol, but if his parents' hidden surprise was stashed on one of them, it couldn't be very big. Which meant it was going to take them even longer to find it.

"Or it could be buried somewhere on the property," Sander added. "And if that's the case, we might have to hire a backhoe or something."

"Maybe we should hire someone with a metal detector to look around for it," Kelsey said.

Her dad brightened at that. "Or maybe I could buy a metal detector and do it myself."

And boom, the rest of Sander's summer—and a good bit of his fall—was planned, Roth thought with a smile. His uncle had never encountered a bit of machinery or technology he hadn't taken a liking to.

"Who's metal detecting?"

Roth turned at the question to find his brother, Harris, coming down the stairs from the second floor. He resembled their uncle far more than Roth did. His blond hair was cropped short and neat, however, and his eyes

were more green than hazel. But like the rest of the Fortune men, he topped six feet, too. Great. Now there were
going to be two metal detectorists out there, because
Harris loved stuff like that almost as much as Sander
did. The only thing he loved more was rodeos.

"Hey, maybe we could *all* get metal detectors," Roth
deadpanned. "We could cover this whole property in...
what? Two, three years? Yeah, that'll work. But only
if the treasure is metal. Which it may or may not be."

Harris made a sour face. "Well, I don't know what
else we're supposed to do. It would help if we knew
something about what Mom and Dad hid around here."

"Oooh, maybe we could hold a séance," Roth heard
Priscilla say as she came down the stairs to join their
brother on the landing. "Ask Mom and Dad to give us
some hints."

Roth smiled at that. Hadn't he just been wishing he
could talk to his folks again? Maybe this was a sign.

"Has anyone looked hard in Mom and Dad's old bedroom?" Zara asked as she came through the door Sander
had passed through moments ago. "Maybe they made a
map to the hiding place before they left for California.
That would make sense, right? Kids love having maps
to follow. So maybe they made one with an actual X-
marks-the-spot that's still in their room somewhere."

That *did* kind of make sense, Roth couldn't help
thinking. His parents, their mom especially, would have
absolutely been likely to do something like that to make
a fun game for their family even more fun.

But Priscilla groaned at their sister's suggestion. "So
now you're saying we might have *two* things to look for."

All of them grumbled at that. Until Sander pointed out that it was past time for dinner, so they might as well just give up looking for today. They could try again tomorrow. And the next day. And so on.

August was going to be a long month.

The family shuffled into the kitchen to find not only Sander's chili, but a pan of jalapeño corn bread waiting. After helping themselves to generous portions of both, they trooped into the dining room and sat in the same chairs at the long table they'd occupied since childhood. As always, the chairs at each end—the ones where Mark and Marlene used to sit—remained empty. The Fortune children had tried to convince Sander to take their dad's chair the first year they all came to Emerald Ridge without their parents, since he was their legal guardian now. But he had flatly refused, claiming his regular spot at what would have been his brother's immediate right. Roth had always sat directly across from Sander, his father's third-in-command.

"So has there been any progress in the investigation into Linc's murder?" Roth asked as he reached for one of the six different hot sauces that were always on the table. Each of the Fortunes had their own favorite, and they did live in Texas, after all.

"Not really," Harris told him. "Though it sounds like Emerald Ridge PD has now spoken to just about everyone in town who knew him."

"That could be all ten thousand residents," Zara said.

Roth knew she was only half joking. Linc Banning had had the kind of personality where he made friends everywhere he went. Roth still couldn't imagine anyone having a beef with him that would make them want to kill him.

"He was either in the wrong place at the wrong time," Harris said, "or else he somehow got involved with something he shouldn't have. I can't think of any other reason why he would have ended up shot to death in the river."

"It had to be the wrong-place-wrong-time thing," Priscilla said. "Linc was too good a guy to get involved with anything sketchy."

"Well, yeah, he was back when we knew him," Kelsey interjected. "He was such a sweet, shy, quiet kid. But none of us has really seen much of him or talked to him for a long time. Oh, except you, Priscilla," she added with a pointed smile for her cousin.

"One time," Priscilla reminded them. "I only went out with him once. And he barely said a word about what he'd been up to these days. He seemed like the old Linc to me, though. Maybe not as quiet or shy as he used to be, but certainly still sweet. I can't believe he got involved with anything shady, either. It would just be so unlike him."

The conversation about Linc's murder dominated their dinner conversation, then followed them out onto the patio after that, where they each took their places around the firepit. Roth had brought a case of Fortune's Vintages Malbec with him for the family to enjoy—the first vintage under the vineyard's new label—and he popped a cork on a couple of bottles for them to share. As the sun began to make its descent toward the trees, talk of Linc Banning gradually ebbed. What replaced it, though, was something Roth wanted to think and talk about even less.

"So how's Antonia Leonetti doing?" Priscilla asked the group at large. Somehow, though, she only seemed to be looking at him.

"Oh, my God," Kelsey added, "can you imagine going through what she did with Charles Cabot? And then having the whole town talking about it after the fact? Plus having to cancel an entire wedding that was barely a month away? I feel so bad for her."

"I couldn't figure out why she was dating that jerk in the first place," Zara threw in. "He was such a bully when we were kids."

Which she well knew, Roth thought. It took years after Cabot pushed her into the pool before Zara was comfortable around water.

"I don't think Antonia ever knew what a dirtbag Charles was back then," Priscilla said.

"She was always a nice kid," Kelsey added. "She's *still* nice, which is probably why she still didn't see what a dirtbag he is."

"Nice?" Roth echoed. "That woman is an absolute shark in the boardroom."

"Oh, right," Harris said. "You guys are competitors with the wine thing. This is excellent, by the way," he added parenthetically, lifting his glass of Malbec in Roth's direction.

Sander grinned. "Has she sent you a proposal to buy Fortune's Vintages since you got back in town? How many of those blue folders do you have now?"

It was no secret in the family that the Leonettis were

doing their best to get their hands on Roth's favorite venture outside Fortune Capital. Mostly it wasn't a secret because he couldn't stop complaining about it whenever they were all in the same room.

He shook his head. "I have zero blue folders," he told his uncle. "I've sent back every one of them with my rejection. All fifteen of them."

"What a shark," Zara said with a chuckle.

"Antonia doesn't seem like a shark outside the boardroom," Priscilla said sweetly. Still looking at Roth. Still smiling.

"How would you know?" he asked his sister.

Although it was true that Antonia had been anything but shark-like during their conversation Saturday evening, that had only been because she'd been in a vulnerable position after the way Cabot had treated her. And she'd been at home with her kid. That didn't mean she couldn't be a shark in other circumstances, however. Which meant he still had to be on his guard around her the next time he saw her. At her daughter's one-year birthday party. With a theme of My First Rodeo. Surrounded by a bunch of other kids. Probably dressed like miniature cowboys and cowgirls. Oh, yeah. She was for sure going to be a shark that day. He'd better watch his back.

Why had he agreed to go to a child's birthday party anyway? he asked himself for perhaps the hundredth time. And one thrown by one of his biggest professional nemeses?

"I don't know," Priscilla said.

At first Roth thought she was reading his mind and

answering his question to himself, since that was the only reply he could think of, too. Then he realized she was responding to the question he'd asked her.

"She was just really nice to me when I ran into her at ER Grocery yesterday," his sister continued. "She was ordering a cake for her daughter's first birthday party. She said you were going to be a guest."

Every gaze at the table flew to Roth's at that. Just, he was certain, as Priscilla had planned.

"Oh, really?" Harris asked with a grin.

"I thought you detested the Leonettis," Zara said.

"Do tell," Kelsey added.

"Yeah, I'd like to hear this story myself," Sander told him. "'Fess up."

'Fess up about what? Roth wondered. About how he couldn't stop thinking warm thoughts about a woman he'd been so sure for years had nothing but ice in her veins? Or how he, the guy who knew nothing about babies and kids, had actually made one laugh a few nights ago? Or how less than two weeks after leaving his home in Dallas for a vacation with his family, he somehow suddenly felt like he didn't belong in Dallas at all?

"There's nothing to tell," he finally said softly.

"Oh, yes, there is," Priscilla reassured them.

Before he could stop her, his youngest sister launched into the whole sordid story about what he'd overheard at Emerald Ridge Café Saturday morning, and how he'd been the one to put the bug in Antonia's ear that her fiancé was only after her money, because he'd followed up his eavesdropping to investigate Cabot's finances—or lack thereof. Everyone in town knew *some*one had uncovered the truth about Cabot and alerted Antonia to what was going on, but no one knew exactly who. Except for Priscilla, of course. And now the rest of the family.

"Roth was also," Priscilla added, "absolutely furious that Charles not only badmouthed Antonia, but called her adorable baby girl a snot-nosed little rug rat."

At this, the others gasped in varying degrees of outrage.

"Man, that Cabot kid was always meaner than a snake," Sander said with a shake of his head.

Zara nodded her agreement. "Though it figures that him insulting a baby would be the trigger that set Roth off."

"I couldn't just sit there and let him get away with it," Roth said, feeling himself getting riled up all over again. "Plus, he insulted Antonia, too."

"Yeah, but she can take care of herself," Kelsey said. "A baby, on the other hand…"

"You do seem to have a soft spot for kids, big brother," Harris reminded him.

"See? I'm not the only one who realizes you're a total cinnamon roll," Priscilla told him. Again.

"You have always been a sucker around kids, Roth," Sander agreed. "Even when you were a kid yourself. Don't you remember how many times you told me to step aside after your folks died and that you could take care of your brother and sisters yourself?"

He and Sander had indeed been at odds about that when Roth was a kid. But that was because Roth had known his siblings better than his uncle had. And at thirteen, he had honestly thought he could take care of them. Looking back now, he of course knew that that would have been impossible. But his reaction had been out of a sense of duty to his parents and loyalty to his family. Not because he was a sucker. Or a cinnamon roll. Or anything else soft or sticky or sweet.

"I just wanted to do the right thing by Antonia," Roth told them all. "The same way I would hope someone would steer me in the right direction if I was about to make a mistake."

His family reacted by smiling at him some more.

"That was all there was to it," he insisted.

Now they all nodded in addition to smiling.

"Antonia invited me to Georgie's birthday party as a way to say thanks for helping her avoid a huge mistake. And I accepted because—"

He halted. He still wasn't sure why he'd accepted. He could have just told her thanks but no thanks. The last place he wanted to be was a kid's birthday party, where there were bound to be lots of other kids, and where the focus of the event would be on a baby who could barely talk. What kind of right-thinking adult wanted any part of that?

"Yeah, do tell," Priscilla echoed Kelsey's earlier words. "Why *did* you agree to go to a baby's first birthday party hosted by a woman you claim you can't stand?"

Roth growled at her with his best big-brother growl. Priscilla chuckled in response.

"When's the party?" Zara asked.

"Thursday," Roth and Priscilla replied as one.

"What are you going to take for a gift?" Zara wanted to know.

"Gift?" Roth echoed.

Zara laughed. "Yeah, gift. It's a birthday party, Roth. You need to bring a present for the birthday girl."

Right. It had been so long since Roth had been to a birthday party, he'd forgotten about the protocols. And what did one-year-olds need or want, anyway?

"I don't know," he confessed. "I didn't think about it."

Kelsey tapped her watch. "If I were you, I'd start thinking about it now. 'Cause you don't have a lot of time for shopping."

Great. Tomorrow, he was going to have to go out and do something he absolutely abhorred—shop. For a baby, no less. With not a single clue what to get. It was going to be Georgie's first rodeo, he remembered. So he guessed he'd just start there.

Chapter Six

Antonia was doing her best to wipe at a smudge of chocolate cupcake icing that had just joined the splatter of grape soda on the white blouse she'd been dumb enough to put on for a child's birthday party when she heard a familiar voice coming from outside the kitchen door. Georgie's party had barely started, but already chaos reigned out in the backyard of the Leonetti estate. Most of the guests had arrived, and the majority of them were under the age of five thanks to how many parents had explained that they couldn't stay for the party but would for sure be back at four o'clock on the dot before running back out to their car and peeling out as if they were being chased by zombies. Antonia was still a new enough mom not to have realized how many parents saw events like birthday parties as a chance to recapture some of their identity as a normal adult by hitting the nail salon or movie theater or golf course for a few hours of child-free bliss.

Thankfully Georgie's nanny, Kayla, had come to help keep an eye on things. Even better, she was a half decade younger than Antonia and child-free herself, so she was full of energy and patience. Gia and Bella were also in attendance, of course, along with Bella's two kids, who, at eight and ten, were old enough to be effective crowd control for their preschool-age counterparts. Her brother, Leo, and his fiancée, Poppy, were here too with their adopted son, but the engaged couple were still so lovey-dovey together Antonia sometimes wondered if they even saw that there was a whole wide world outside the two of them. And she'd made her mother and grandfather promise to just enjoy themselves at the party and not lift a finger. The remainder of the guests were the children of Antonia's friends and other babies and toddlers Georgie knew through the play groups Kayla had joined for them after coming to work for Antonia when Georgie was three months old. Even with the extra grown-up hands, though, it was going to be a long four hours.

That thought was hammered home when Roth walked through the kitchen door, looking like something from a Hollywood Western. His dark hair gleamed in the midday sun spilling through the window beside him, and his eyes glittered like pale blue gemstones paired with the sage green of his Western-style shirt. He'd rolled back the cuffs to reveal a set of muscular forearms that made a woman want to swoon—evidenced by how light-headed Antonia suddenly felt at the sight of him—and he'd left open the top two buttons to reveal that tantalizing divot at the base of a man's throat that her fingers suddenly itched to trace. Roth had paired the shirt with dark denim jeans, a garment that hugged his hips and thighs with the kind of affection that would make a lover drool.

Not that she was Roth's lover. Ahem. Not that she

wanted to be Roth's lover. Ahem. She just appreciated a good-looking man, nothing more than that. All the moms who'd dropped off their children so hastily were going to regret not being here this afternoon. *Ah-hem.*

"Hi," she said when she saw him.

He dipped his head forward in greeting. "Hi yourself."

She wanted to tell him how thrilled she was to see him, since she was surprisingly happy he was here. Um, because he could be another set of hands to help with the kids, of course. Instead, she only said, "Thank you for coming."

"Thank you for inviting me."

"It's going to be a fun afternoon. I promise."

She wasn't sure if she'd said that for his benefit or her own. As if cued by the comment, however, a trio of high-pitched screams pierced the air from outside the open back door, fairly rattling the dishes in the cabinet behind her. Roth's gaze flew toward where the sound had come from, and Antonia could tell without even looking back that something of the not-good variety must be going on.

He pointed in that direction. "Is it okay for those kids to be hanging upside down from the big acacia back there? And pelting the other kids with silly straws?"

Antonia shook her head. "No. No, it's not."

"Where are their parents?"

"Probably getting a sugar scrub right about now." She hoped she hadn't sounded too envious when she'd said it.

"Sugar scrub?"

He was doubtless thinking it was some kind of party

treat. Which Antonia guessed it kind of was for the moms who weren't at the party.

But she just smiled and told Roth, "Never mind."

She turned around to rescue the acacia tree and the other children from the marauders and was relieved to see Gia and Bella already there, carefully extracting the trio of simian wannabes. It really was going to be a long afternoon.

Roth was great through all of it, though, even donning one of the fuzzy stick-on mustaches and straw cowboy hats provided for each of the guests—the latter of which was about ten sizes too small for him and sat atop his head like a clown hat. The children were delighted by his antics and, Antonia had to admit, so was she. He was great with all the kids, all afternoon, and they all responded to him as if he were one of them. He even won the prize for pin-the-tail-on-the-donkey—a stuffed, lime green horse that made real horsey sounds when its ear was squeezed—which he immediately bestowed upon the second-place winner instead, telling the little girl it was totally okay, because he already had one at home just like it.

Why was this man not already a father? she asked herself more than once that afternoon. He was a natural with kids. Immediately, however, she knew the answer. He'd already told her himself how he didn't want to be in a long-term committed relationship. She understood. Although she'd never considered herself to be commitment-phobic before—on the contrary, she'd fallen too hard too fast on more than one occasion—after what had happened with both Silvio and Charles, she was never going to give her heart to anyone again. The fact that she was already starting to feel warm and fuzzy about Roth on the heels of her broken engagement to Charles told her she was still too quick to see the best in the opposite sex and ignore the worst. No way could she ever trust her feelings again.

The party did, finally, wind down, and Antonia didn't think she'd ever been more exhausted in her life than when she closed the front door behind the last of the guests. She'd assured her mother and grandfather, as well as her siblings and niece and nephew, that she could take it from here, that they'd all gone above and beyond as party chaperones. Then she'd told them all to go into town for dinner on her. Papa declined in favor of turning in early, but the rest of the Leonettis happily complied. When Roth offered to help with the cleanup, she reassured him, too, that she was perfectly able to do it herself. But he insisted. And honestly, when she saw the state of the kitchen, she was happy to have his help.

Together, they made short work of the mess, loading the dishwasher to capacity and filling two garbage bags with paper plates and cups and battered decorations. Then, together, they retreated to the—much less chaotic now—patio, where Antonia opened a bottle of Leonetti Vineyards wine. Though this one—a Médoc— was much less expensive than the vintage they'd shared the other night, it was still one of which her sister Bella was particularly proud.

They had just seated themselves in wide mesh patio chairs when Kayla stepped outside to tell Antonia she'd bathed and fed Georgie and that the baby had conked out in seconds after being put to bed. Antonia wasn't surprised. Her baby girl had seen more excitement today than she'd ever had in her life. She'd probably sleep like a rock tonight, all night. She thanked Kayla again for her help today—the nanny would see a nice bonus in her paycheck this week—and bid her good-night. After rising to switch on one of the ubiquitous baby monitors placed all over the house in case Georgie did wake up fretful, she took her seat next to Roth again and enjoyed a very generous taste of her wine. Oh, yeah, Bella had a good reason to rave about this one. She leaned back in her chair, closed her eyes and sighed.

When she heard Roth chuckle beside her, she opened one eye to look at him. "What?" she said.

"I was thinking you look like a woman who's just survived being lost at sea for a month."

She opened her other eye. "Don't be silly. If I'd been lost at sea, I wouldn't have been able to pig out on cake and ice cream all day."

And she wouldn't be wearing a blouse spattered with a dozen other stains now—everything from grass to blood. Not her own, thankfully, but little Zayn Hayek's knee was going to be sporting that cowboy Band-Aid for the rest of the day.

Roth grinned. "I honestly can't remember the last time I had cake and ice cream. Not at the same time, anyway. That's just such a birthday party thing."

"What? You Fortunes don't have birthday parties?" she asked, feigning horror.

"Of course we do," he assured her. "When we're all in the same place at the same time on someone's birthday. But that doesn't happen as often these days as it did when we were kids. And the whole cake and ice cream thing kind of got replaced by charcuterie and chicken wings."

"Party poopers."

Now he laughed. "Yeah, I guess adulting doesn't include nearly as much sugar as childhood did. And here we thought it was going to be such a great gig when we were kids."

Well, that was unfortunately true. Antonia still couldn't believe how hard she'd fought naps when she was little. She'd do anything now for a chance to grab some midday shut-eye.

"But it does have some perks," she said. "It's nice not having to be home before dark. And the weekly allowance is a lot better."

Roth raised his glass to that. "And I don't have to cut the grass to earn it."

Antonia lifted her wine flute, too. "For me, it was doing the laundry. Each one of us had a specific chore we were responsible for in addition to the smaller ones we all shared. To this day, I always add something dark in with the light load as an act of rebellion." Vehemently, she added, *"Because I can."*

He chuckled again. "Yeah, when I was a kid, I always deliberately missed one little patch by the petunias. Used to drive my dad nuts." He looked skyward. "Sorry, Dad."

Antonia's heart pinched tight. She hadn't known Roth or his brother or sisters well when they were kids, but everyone in Emerald Ridge knew their history. She couldn't imagine coping with the deaths of both her mother and father. At the same time, no less. And certainly not when she was as young as the Fortunes had been. She made a mental note to hug her mother tight when her family returned from town.

"We lost our dad, too," Antonia said softly. "Ten years ago."

Roth met her gaze. "I remember. I'm sorry."

"I'm sorry about your folks, too."

"Thanks."

"It was a plane crash, wasn't it?"

Roth nodded, his brows arrowing downward at what was obviously still a painful memory. "With my dad at the wheel. He was a great pilot, but there was a freak storm over the San Bernardino Mountains that came out of nowhere. They were on their way back from flying to Los Angeles to scope out a minor league baseball team they were thinking about buying." His melancholy expression softened with clear affection. "The Moreno Valley Jackdaws. My parents were both huge baseball fans. Harris and I used to be, too, before the accident. The whole family had season tickets for the Texas Rangers. Even my uncle Sander and cousin Kelsey. And why am I telling you all this?" he finished with an exasperated sound. "You can't possibly be interested in any of that."

"No, it's okay," she assured him. She told herself she was only being polite. But courtesy had nothing to do with it. For some reason, she was really interested in what he was telling her. Maybe because, somewhere deep down, she really wanted to learn as much as she could about Roth?

He threw her a halfhearted smile, then dropped his

gaze down to his boot, stubbing the toe of it against the creekstone patio. "Thanks, Antonia. That's nice of you. It's weird, but none of us has attended any Ranger games for years. We usually give the tickets to friends. It's just not the same without Mom and Dad, you know?"

She nodded. "I don't think it's weird at all, and I do know. My mom and dad always took us kids to Big Bend Park every summer, to camp and hike and just breathe in the great outdoors. That all stopped when he got sick. None of us has been there since. None of us ever even talks about wanting to go again."

Whenever the siblings had tried to make plans to go after their father's death, something had always come up with at least one of them. Certainly none of them was as footloose as they had been when they were young, but the real reason was that it just wouldn't have been the same without their dad.

"Change isn't always a good thing," she said softly.

"No, it's not," Roth agreed.

"And sometimes you just want to remember the good times as good, with no sadness tainting them."

He nodded but said nothing. They each ruminated in silence for a long moment, gazing at the sky, where the sun was beginning to dip low toward the vineyard. But Antonia didn't want a day of celebration to be ending with thoughts of melancholy. Her daughter had just passed a major milestone. Georgie was one! How had an entire year gone by since her birth?

"Thank you for Georgie's present," she told Roth softly. "It was very thoughtful. Not to mention extremely generous."

He looked grateful for the change of subject. "Well, you did say this was her first rodeo," he reminded her. "I just wanted to get her started with a bang."

That he had certainly done.

"She's going to love it," Antonia assured him. Once she was a teenager and could fit into it. "Every girl needs a saddle."

And the one Roth had bought for Georgie was about as top-of-the-line as they came, with exquisite leather work and more bells and whistles than she would ever use, unless she became a professional rodeo rider.

"My brother, Harris, helped me pick it out. I know we're all Texans, but I, at least, am not particularly horsey. Harris, on the other hand, would spend every waking moment at the rodeo if he could."

Well, that explained the bells and whistles. "The horse gene is strong in the Leonetti DNA," Antonia assured him. "Not as strong as the wine gene, but Bella and Gia and I all read every horse book we could get our hands on as kids, and my whole bedroom décor before I discovered K-pop was all horses, all the time."

"Do you still ride?"

"I do," she told him. "We have three horses stabled here at the vineyard. Bella likes to check out the grapes on horseback, and Leo's fiancée, Poppy, is super horsey. I try to ride every weekend if I can find time. Georgie's actually already been out with me some mornings in the Snugli. Always easy rides, of course, but she really likes it, too. I'm sure she'll be asking for a pony for Christmas every year, just like I did until I got one."

Roth looked relieved to know that his gift to her

daughter would not go unused. Then he smiled. "Do you still listen to K-pop?"

Antonia smiled back. "Maybe."

Their conversation lightened a lot after that, and they talked about the sorts of things people talked about when they were getting to know each other better. Not that she and Roth Fortune were getting deeply acquainted or anything. They were just making superficial, meaningless conversation after a long, exhausting day. She was about to ask him if he wanted another glass of wine when the sound of Georgie crying erupted from the baby monitor behind them.

"Be right back," she told Roth as she leaped up from her chair to head back into the house.

"Do you want me to come, too?"

"No, that's okay," she called over her shoulder. "Pour us a couple more glasses. I'll just be a minute."

She hoped. But just as had been the case with Georgie on other nights, try as she might to soothe her daughter, she was inconsolable. Since Kayla had fed her before putting her to bed, and Georgie's diaper was dry, she knew neither hunger nor wetness could be the reason for her distress. It might be the teething, or she might be overstimulated after such a big day. Or maybe she was crying for another reason entirely, one that Antonia couldn't figure out. She'd spoken to the pediatrician about these bouts of night crying, and Georgie's doctor hadn't been concerned. Lots of babies just went through periods of crying, she'd told Antonia. Her baby was happy and healthy. There was no cause for alarm.

Except that she was alarmed. Who wouldn't be when their baby was crying and they couldn't calm her down?

"Everything okay up here?"

She turned to find Roth framed in the nursery doorway, much as he had been that first night when he was here. Just as he had been then, he was bathed in the soft blues of the nursery nightlight, a softly turning carousel lamp that threw stars along the walls and ceiling—and now on Roth, too. Just as he had then, he looked hesitant to enter. And just as she had been then, Antonia was more than a little relieved to have him here with her.

"Not really," she said over her daughter's crying. "Everything should be fine. She's not wet, there's nothing scary, and she can't be hungry already. There's never anything wrong that I can see when she cries like this. I don't understand why she's upset. Again."

Roth took a few hesitant steps forward, though whether that was because he wasn't sure if he was intruding or if he was intimidated by Georgie's caterwauling, she couldn't have said. When Antonia offered no indication that she wanted him to leave, though, he hastened his step forward, stopping beside her to look down at the baby.

The second her daughter saw him over her shoulder, her crying eased. Then, after a moment, it ceased completely. Her brown eyes still welled with tears, and her little lip continued to tremble, but she stopped bawling to fix her gaze on Roth's face.

"Hello there, Miz Georgie," he said in soft voice. "How you doin', li'l cowgirl?"

Georgie hiccupped once, but never stopped looking at

Roth. His eyes never left hers, either. Slowly, she raised
a hand toward him, her chubby little fingers uncurl-
ing, until her index finger was extended more than the
rest. When Antonia turned her head to look at Roth, he
was smiling at the baby. Then, he leaned forward over
her shoulder until Georgie could—and did—grab his
nose. At that, the baby made a soft sound of satisfaction,
then laughed. Then looked at her mother as if making
sure she wasn't overstepping some social boundary she
hadn't even learned about yet.

But Antonia was too busy being distracted by Roth's
nearness to send her daughter a reassuring cue. How
could she be comforting when she was suddenly a bundle of nerves that had nothing to do with her daughter
and everything to do with the heat and scent of Roth,
whose body and face were by now nearly flush against
her own? Holy smokes, the man smelled good, a mix of
balsam and sage and campfire, with a hint of birthday
cake that was irresistible. It was all she could do not to
tilt her head to the right, to press her cheek against his.

Fortunately, his focus was still on Georgie, so he was
oblivious to the shudders of heat and desire and need
winding through her. When he laughed, Georgie's gaze
flew back to his, and she laughed with him. Then Antonia's tangle of odd feelings for Roth turned into surprise when her daughter reached out both arms toward
him. Georgie had never reached for anyone before. Not
even one of the Leonettis. Certainly she loved her aun-
ties and uncle and grandmother and great-grandfather
and reveled in their affectionate hugs. But as eagerly as
she had participated, she'd never been the one to insti-

gate the embraces. Maybe that was just because she'd never needed to. It was still surprising to see Georgie reach so easily for Roth.

He looked as stunned as Antonia was to have her daughter asking for him to hold her. He arched his brows in silent question to Antonia and lifted his own arms toward the baby. Clearly, he wasn't as reluctant about taking her now as he had been Friday night. After only a moment's hesitation, she settled Georgie into his arms. It took a moment for him to arrange his stance and himself to get the baby into a comfortable hold, but he instinctively began to rock Georgie slowly back and forth, never taking his eyes from her face once.

"What's got you troubled, little one?" he asked the baby. "Did you have too much cake and ice cream?"

Georgie cooed at that, then babbled something only she could understand. Roth laughed anyway, as if he understood her pithy comments completely. "I know, right? There's no such thing as too much cake and ice cream. So what has you so shook up?"

The baby jabbered again, a bunch of incoherent syllables that Roth met with a sage nod. "I see. Well, there's no reason to be upset over something like that. Life is gonna be full of things you don't like. You just have to let 'em go."

Georgie's eyebrows knitted downward, as if she'd understood him completely and was giving his advice much consideration. Then she prattled something else. Once again, Roth listened with much interest, his gaze never leaving hers.

"Well, I guess you're right about that," he told the

baby. "Some things are hard to let go of. Just try not to let them get the better of you."

Georgie murmured her agreement, then the two of them enjoyed a bit more back-and-forth. Antonia watched with amazement. Even she didn't have conversations this long with her daughter. Mostly because Georgie lost interest fairly quickly whenever Antonia tried. With Roth, though, the baby hung on every word. Obviously, he spoke infant way better than Antonia did.

As their conversation wound down, Georgie's eyes began to grow heavy, until they closed completely. Roth looked at Antonia, clearly in silent question about what he should do. Instead of taking her daughter from him, she pointed silently at the crib. He looked a little panicked by the idea of moving anywhere with a baby in his arms, but she smiled with encouragement and stepped close to his side, curling one arm through his and the other under her sleeping daughter—and doing her best to ignore the ribbon of heat that wound through her with even that simple bodily contact with his. Together, they inched slowly to the side of the crib, then Roth bent with excruciating care to place Georgie at its center. The baby resettled herself on her tummy but never opened her eyes. Antonia waited to see if she would erupt again, but she only sighed and fell into a deeper sleep.

She threw Roth a grateful smile, then pointed toward the nursery door, and they both crept out, literally on tiptoe, so as not to wake Georgie. Once they were in the hall, she realized she still had her arm looped through his and that their bodies were still moving together as one, fluidly and easily, as if they walked through the house this way together all the time. Hastily, she withdrew her arm from his, then carefully closed the door behind them...then battled the impulse to link their arms together again. She waited a few beats to make sure that the soft click of the door didn't wake Georgie up again, then pointed toward the stairs.

By the time they were settled back in their chairs on the patio, the sun had disappeared over the horizon, and the sky was smudged with the soft amethyst of twilight. The moon was rising over the distant hills, and a handful of fireflies were warming up for their nightly calling. Antonia poured them each another glass of wine, and they settled back to enjoy more quiet conversation.

The only problem at that point was that neither of them seemed to have a clue what to say.

Chapter Seven

Roth and Antonia gazed out at the evening that was darkening the sky behind her house as if they were both seeing nightfall for the first time. Antonia sipped her wine. He sipped his. But neither looked at the other or uttered a word.

Until, finally, he split the silence with a quietly offered, "Maybe she's just lonely."

Antonia knew he was talking about Georgie, but there was something in the comment that she felt deep in her soul. She opened her mouth to deny it—both on her own behalf, and on behalf of her daughter—then closed it again. Antonia wasn't lonely. She wasn't. She had a big family and lots of friends. Until Friday, she'd been engaged to a man she had thought would be in her life forever. How could she possibly be bereft when she was surrounded by people who loved her? Even if, sometimes, she admittedly did kind of feel lonely. That happened to everyone sometimes.

Right?

With Georgie, though, well… She'd never thought about the possibility that her daughter might be lonely. She was never by herself when she was awake. Nighttime was the only time Georgie was truly alone. But if loneliness was the case, why wasn't she comforted by her mother's presence? Why was it that only Roth seemed to have the magic touch?

Antonia looked over at him again. He'd been great with all the kids at the party. Maybe there was just some kind of natural aura around some people that kids recognized and responded to. Maybe having such pure souls, they were able to see things in others that grown-ups, with their decades of bombardment with learning and socializing, couldn't see. Maybe it was just the fact that Roth was a good guy, and Georgie was able to see that.

Which would also explain why her daughter had never really taken to Charles. Maybe Georgie had been able to see what Antonia couldn't—that he wasn't a good guy.

"I don't think Georgie is lonely," Antonia finally said after giving Roth's suggestion more thought. "She's been sleeping in a room by herself since she was three months old, and she used to wake up during the night with no problem and put herself back to sleep. It's only been the past couple of months that she's been crying at night like this."

Since Antonia had gotten engaged, she couldn't help thinking now. Maybe, on some subconscious level, she had been having misgivings about Charles all along. Maybe Georgie had picked up on those misgivings, even when Antonia hadn't seen them herself. Or maybe it had just been the stress of wedding planning and now the upheaval of her breakup with Charles. Hopefully once Antonia worked through all her conflicting, confounding emotions, Georgie would settle down, too. Though that still didn't explain why the baby responded to Roth the way she did.

"But I do think," she added, because she couldn't help herself, "that Georgie definitely stops crying specifically because of you."

He looked flummoxed by that. "Nah, that's not possible. She doesn't even know me. That first night I was here, she'd never even seen me before."

"All the more reason to believe it's your appearance, especially, that calms her down. You just have a way with kids."

He shook his head more vehemently. "No way. I'm just a distraction to Georgie, that's all. Something new that she has to stop whatever she's doing and figure out. I have no idea what I'm doing with kids because I've never been around them before. And I have no desire to have any of my own," he hurried on when he saw her about to object, "I'm a businessman. I'm pragmatic. I do business. Pragmatic business. There's no room for children in my world."

Antonia tried hard to bite back her laughter at the lengths he was going to convince her, and himself, too, that he was way too businesslike and pragmatic to be in any way child-friendly. Tried...and failed. Although she didn't guffaw in his face, she did enjoy a brief chuckle.

"You don't have to have any idea about how to act around children," she told him. "You learn as you go." Which had been the case with her. "But for some people, it's an innate instinct, and that's obviously what's happening with you. You're just naturally good with kids, Roth. And kids recognize that, even if you don't."

He opened his mouth, obviously to argue, then closed it again and shook his head. "You couldn't be more wrong," he said.

She didn't push it, even though she knew she was right. Why Roth couldn't see what was obvious, Antonia couldn't say. But he *was* good with kids. And it was kind of a shame he never intended to have any of his own. He really would be a wonderful father.

They turned their conversation to less personal matters after that, finishing their wine with talk of a new tech startup Roth had great hopes for, and a new blended white vintage Bella was currently working on, and how surprisingly pleasant the late summer evenings had been so far. By the time they finished, the moon had made a full appearance, and a handful of stars were scattered across the now indigo sky.

When Roth uttered his need to get going, Antonia was hit by an unexpected pang of regret. Only because it had been a while since she'd enjoyed such nice conversation with anyone besides her family. Then she remembered how many conversations she and Charles had shared before she realized what a jerk he was. Yes, they'd discussed combining work-life balance for two people instead of one, and parenting Georgie, and how they were going to share their finances after they were married—that last part had been especially important to Charles. But all those discussions had centered on rules and outlines and expectations. Not once could she remember telling her now ex-fiancé about how much she missed vacationing with her family at Big Bend or how her favorite books when she was growing up were all in the Saddle Club series.

"Thanks for a fun day," Roth said now as he rose from his chair.

He arched his back into a long stretch to counter the effects of being stationary for so long, lifting his arms over his head to work out the kinks. Antonia tried very hard, really she did, not to notice how his actions seemed to flex every muscle he possessed, from his strong forearms to his broad shoulders to his sturdy chest and firm back to his narrow waist and trim hips. And seriously, he must have an amazing anatomy, she couldn't help thinking as she watched him. Because the way his shirt strained against his torso and the way his jeans hugged his legs, and the way she wanted to stand up in that moment and close the short distance between them and just…taste him…all over made her wonder if there was any way that—

"Antonia?"

The sound of her name seemed to come at her from a million miles away, permeating the haze and fog of some weird sexual awakening she seemed to be suddenly having, and her gaze flew to Roth's.

Oh, crap. Had he been able to tell what she was thinking about? How could she have been thinking about that in the first place? Surely, she hadn't spoken any of that out loud. Had she…?

"Are you okay?" he asked.

She nodded, a ragged, jittery gesture. She couldn't help it. She was feeling ragged and jittery. And also kind of…aroused? Oh, surely not. She was just feeling the effects of the wine. Yeah, that was it. She made a mental note to tell Bella tomorrow how the wine tasting with Roth tonight had been *sooo goood*. Except she wouldn't make it sound as sexual as it did in her head.

Um, where was she? Right. About to say goodnight to Roth. And not a moment too soon.

"It's good," she said. "Uh, I mean I'm fine," she quickly amended. "Just starting to feel the effects of the day. I need to get to…" *Do not tell him you need to get to bed*, she commanded herself. Because there was no way, in her current state, that it wouldn't sound like a come-on. "I need to get some sleep," she managed instead.

He nodded. "Right there with you."

Oh, she really wished he hadn't used that particular phrase. Now she was picturing him in bed with her. Doing things she should absolutely not be picturing him doing between the sheets with her.

She jumped up from her chair with all the speed and grace of a rhinoceros and told him she'd see him out. The sooner the better. They stopped long enough in the kitchen to set their glasses and what was left of the wine on the counter when something on the kitchen desk caught her attention. A dark blue folder Leo had brought over for her to give to Roth. A new proposal he'd put together to buy Fortune's Vintages after Antonia told him she'd invited Roth to Georgie's party. Leo had figured that since she and Roth were becoming friends—even though she had assured her brother that she was *not* friends with Roth Fortune, that he was, in fact, still the Leonettis' *most dangerous professional enemy* who just really liked cake and ice cream—then maybe Roth would be more amenable to a new offer from them to sell.

She expelled a weary sigh and went to retrieve the folder, then returned and extended it to Roth. Who immediately knew what it was and started shaking his head before she even reached him.

"I can't believe you'd use your daughter's birthday party to do business," he said.

Frankly, Antonia couldn't believe it, either. But she'd never hear the end of it from the rest of her family if she didn't give it to him after telling them she would…once they'd finally stopped badgering her about it. "Leo put it together," she told him wearily. "Just read it. You might like the conditions this time."

"Thanks, but no thanks," he replied. "I'm not selling Fortune's Vintages. To the Leonettis or anyone else."

Antonia set the folder on the counter. "I'll have it couriered over to you tomorrow."

"Don't waste your money. I'll courier it right back." He threw her a small grin. "And then I'll bill you for the expense."

She wondered what it would take to get Roth to change his mind about selling. They'd already offered him more than the going rate. Tonight, though, was not the night to be making deals. She'd done what she promised her family she would do, and she would have it delivered to him tomorrow. After that, it was out of her hands. At least until one of them could put together another proposal he might find more tempting.

They made their way through the house to the front door, and Antonia tugged it open. Enough darkness had crept into the sky by now that the front porch light had come on. As Roth stepped over the threshold, the pale yellow from the lamp bathed him in amber, giving him the appearance of a golden god. He felt like a god to her at the moment. She might never have gotten Georgie settled back down tonight if it weren't for him. Which meant she never would have gotten to sleep herself. And after a day like today…

She just felt mellow and calm in that moment, two things she hadn't felt for a very long time. She owed Roth for that, too, she supposed, after he was such a nice distraction this evening. It was getting to the point where she wondered if she would ever be able to repay him for all the ways he'd helped her in the last week. They were standing nearly toe-to-toe on the front porch, and, without even thinking about what she was doing, Antonia leaned forward and brushed a kiss over his cheek. Roth looked as surprised by the gesture as she was, lifting a hand to place his fingertips over the spot where her lips had touched his skin.

"What was that for?" he said, his voice low and rough.

Honestly, she wasn't sure. She only knew in that moment that he deserved a reward for all the work he'd done today. Not just calming down Georgie a little while ago but being so great with all the kids at the party. And then helping her clean up afterward. And then being so comfortable and pleasant to talk to. In spite of having been married to one man and engaged to another, Antonia couldn't remember ever feeling around a man the way she had tonight. Comfortable. Easy. Wistful.

Which was weird, since she should be nursing a broken heart and fretting about Georgie's nighttime crying and worrying about all the work she needed to catch up on in light of how much she'd neglected things with wedding planning and canceling. But, in that moment, she wasn't particularly troubled about any of it. There was something about Roth that put her mind at ease, even if only temporarily.

"It was for being a good guy," she finally told him, pushing all her other thoughts away. Because those were thoughts she shouldn't be having. Not when he was on her doorstep, looking more handsome than any man had a right to be.

Sleep, she reminded herself. She needed sleep. Tomorrow, she would feel normal again, and Roth would stop seeming so wonderful and go back to being her professional nemesis. He would. Really. She was sure of it.

They were still standing close, and the light around them was still golden and otherworldly. An owl hooted somewhere in the distance, and fireflies danced all over the yard behind him. The wind kicked up, nudging a stray strand of hair over her forehead, and Roth reached forward with the hand that wasn't holding his hat to gently push it back behind her ear. Then he was leaning toward her this time, and then somehow, he was kissing her. Only not on the cheek. On the lips. And suddenly, Antonia was kissing him right back.

It wasn't a passionate kiss. But it was enough to stir something to life inside her that made her wish that it was. Roth's lips brushed over hers once, twice, three times, each a little more insistent than the one before it. She lifted a hand to cup his cheek in her palm, and he dropped his hand to her waist, curling his fingers over her hip. For one brief, lovely moment, they only enjoyed the kiss, the twilight, the soft breeze, and each other. Then, as suddenly as they had leaned in, they both pulled back. Though they didn't separate. With his hand still curved over her hip, Roth pressed his forehead to hers, and Antonia moved her hand from his cheek to his shoulder. Neither said a word, only gazed down at the ground, as if neither had any idea what to say. Then, with much reluctance, she removed her hand and took a step backward, until he was forced to drop his hand to his side, too.

She tried to look at him, but couldn't, and instead drove her gaze to the night sky. But she wasn't quite able to keep herself from murmuring, very softly, "Wow."

He seemed no more able to look at her when he agreed, "Yeah."

For another moment, they only avoided each other's gazes and said nothing. Then Antonia tried again.

"That, um…" She stopped when she realized she was struggling as much with her words as she was with her thoughts. Finally, she told him, "That, ah… We probably shouldn't have done that."

"No," he agreed roughly, "we probably shouldn't have."

"I'm not sure what came over me."

"Me neither."

"It just kind of happened."

"It did."

Unbidden—and unflinchingly—their gazes finally connected again. As much as he'd just agreed with her that the kiss had been a mistake, he looked like he wanted to lean in for another one. And as wrong as it was, she kind of hoped he would.

"So what are we going to do about it?" he asked her.

She wished she had a good answer for that. Unfortunately, her brain seemed to be well and truly done with thinking for the day. Because the only response it was giving her was to kiss him again. Weave her fingers through his dark hair. And unfasten the buttons on his shirt to dip her hand inside and trace her fingertips over every inch of hard muscle beneath, from his deltoids to his obliques. She caught her breath as a ribbon of heat uncurled inside her. And then she wanted to unbuckle his belt and lower his zipper so that she could drive her hand even lower, down to his—

"I have no idea," she lied. In a husky voice she didn't even recognize as her own.

Roth seemed to notice the change in her timbre, too, because his eyes grew dark with desire.

"It really shouldn't have happened," she reiterated. Not just for him, but for herself, too. "It's just been a long day, and a long week, and I'm exhausted, and—"

He nodded. "And I'm only in town long enough to commemorate the twentieth anniversary of my parents' deaths and deal with the murder of a friend."

She nodded, rushing to add, "Plus we're both on the rebound, and—"

"And neither of us should be pursuing anything with anyone when we're both in a weird place emotionally."

She was relieved that he understood and agreed. Even if she was also a little frustrated by it. She really did have no business kissing someone less than a week after her breakup with Charles...which had come barely a year after her divorce from Silvio. Twice now, she'd been burned by someone she had been certain she would spend the rest of her life with. And completely misjudged someone she'd been sure would love her forever. It didn't matter how wonderful Roth had been today. She needed time—a *lot* of time, honestly—to sort herself out and figure out why she kept being drawn to men who broke her heart before she could even begin to think about starting a new relationship. With anyone.

And Roth was right about his own situation, too. His feelings must be pretty raw right now, remembering his parents' deaths and striving to come to terms with the violent murder of a childhood friend. Their kiss tonight had only come about because they were both in a place where they were struggling emotionally and reaching out for any comfort they could find. She supposed neither of them should be surprised by what had just happened. But they both needed to make sure it never happened again.

She was about to tell him all this, even though she was pretty sure he was thinking the same thing, when they both heard the sound of the Leonetti Vineyards SUV coming up the long drive from the other side of the trees. The last thing either of them needed was to be caught by her family looking like they'd just been

kissing on the front porch. Roth seemed to agree, because he quickly took a few steps backward. They had
just enough time to compose themselves when the ve-
hicle came to a halt at the foot of the steps, and her family tumbled out.

The kids were the first to arrive on the porch, clearly
amped up by the best dessert they'd ever had—*Seriously,
Aunt Antonia, you have* got *to try the new lemon icebox
cake at Francesca's Bar and Grill, it is* so *good!*—but
were quickly joined by Bella and Gia and their mother,
Martina, who, judging by their expressions, weren't
nearly as fooled as the kids were by Antonia's assur-
ances that she and Roth had just been out here talking
about what a fun day it had been for Georgie and what
a nice night it was now, but they were just about to say
goodbye before Mr. Fortune had to head home. *Oh and
wasn't it nice of Mr. Fortune to help me clean up that
huge post-party mess? He is such a good guy.*

When she looked past her niece and nephew to see
her sisters and mother still standing at the foot of the
stairs grinning like idiots, she knew that none of them
had been fooled by her story at all. In fact, her mother
was shaking her head softly in that *What have you done
now, Antonia?* way she had always done whenever she'd
caught her hiding in the pantry with brownies still warm
from the oven, the pan already half-empty.

"That *was* nice of Mr. Fortune," Bella agreed in the
Oh, sure, it is voice that she'd perfected with her own
kids.

"*Super* nice," Gia concurred. "Wow, it must have
been even messier than we realized when we left, if

you guys are just now saying good-night." With a knowing smile that rivaled Bella's dubious tone of voice, she added, "You shouldn't have been in such a hurry to chase us all off."

Bella nodded. "We would have been happy to help, and then Roth could have had a nice quiet evening at home."

Yeah, yeah, yeah.

Antonia turned to Roth, crossing her arms over her midsection, assuring herself she was *not* doing it in order to keep her hands to herself. It was just a little chilly out here for August, that was all.

"Thank you again for all your help, Roth," she said. "I couldn't have done it without you."

Bella and Gia both laughed quietly. Her mother just kept smiling. But they all had the decency to climb the stairs and go inside with softly muttered thanks and farewells to Roth, guiding the children in ahead of them, to leave the two of them alone. Well, as alone as they could be with two nosy sisters, a knowing mother and a couple of oblivious kids milling about, since any of them could spring up again unannounced.

Antonia sighed softly, then lowered her voice. "Like they all said, it was nice of you to stay and help, Roth. Thank you again."

"It was my pleasure," he murmured. Then he smiled when he realized what a double entendre he'd just uttered. "All of it. Was my pleasure."

The kiss had been her pleasure, too. But it still shouldn't have happened.

"Well," she said. But she didn't know what to add.

"Well," Roth echoed. But he didn't seem to know what else to say, either.

"I guess I'll see you when I see you," she finally told him.

"I'll be around," he assured her.

Antonia nodded, then watched with mixed emotions as he finally made his way to the steps and strode down them. Once he was on the ground, he turned around again. "Good night," he told her.

"Good night," she replied. "Drive safe."

Roth lifted his Stetson in farewell, then crossed to where he'd parked his car. Antonia stayed on the porch as he started the engine and pulled away, then kept standing there until his red taillights were out of sight. When she turned around, she halfway expected to see her sisters and mother standing framed in the doorway, smiling their knowing smiles. But they were gone, too, and Antonia was all alone with the twilit night falling around her.

No, not alone, she reassured herself. Georgie was sleeping upstairs, her sisters were prowling around, and her niece and nephew were probably in the family room, loading up whatever game had taken their fancy most recently. Papa was doubtless already in bed asleep, and their mother was almost certainly in the library looking for something to read. The house was full of people, full of life, full of love. There was absolutely no reason why Antonia should feel alone.

She looked down the long road Roth Fortune had just driven. No reason at all, she told herself again. So why, with a house full of people behind her, did she suddenly feel as if she were the only person in the world?

Chapter Eight

After what had easily been the most exhausting day in recent memory, Roth lay wide awake in bed in the house his parents had built for him, staring at the ceiling. Just what the hell had that kiss with Antonia been about? Okay, sure, it was obvious the two of them liked each other. And yeah, they'd had a nice evening chatting once the chaos of the day was over and before Georgie woke up. But she was still his adversary when it came to Fortune's Vintages. And although he certainly enjoyed more than one friendly rivalry with a competing business, he'd sure as hell never kissed that business rival.

Then again, Antonia had been the one to kiss him, hadn't she? At least the first time. But that one had been sweet and chaste and given in fatigued gratitude. It was the second one that had turned into something neither one of them had seen coming. And he'd been the one to initiate it, even if she had joined in very nicely.

She was right, though, that neither of those kisses should have happened. And he was glad that they were both in agreement that nothing like that would transpire again. Professional conflicts aside, they both also had a lot on their plates right now. He was coping with memories of his parents and still reeling over what had happened to Linc, so not in the best place emotionally. And she was dealing with an only-days-old broken engagement that had left her with a bunch of turbulent emotions. He knew what it was like to be involved with someone then suddenly not involved. The sudden change in circumstances could leave a person feeling a million different things and wondering about a million more, not the least of which was just what exactly they wanted from life anyway.

But he liked being single, he reminded himself. He did. Most of the time anyway. And he didn't even mind being alone. For some reason, though, lying there in bed staring at the ceiling, he suddenly felt more than alone. He felt kind of…bereft. As if he were actually missing some piece of himself. Which was bizarre, because he was a man who had it all. Loving family, thriving business, luxurious and mortgage-free home, lots of money in the bank. He wasn't missing anything in his life. Not one single thing. So why did he suddenly feel as if a big gaping hole had just ripped itself open?

He looked at the clock. It was after two, and he hadn't slept a wink. As tired as he was, he wasn't sleepy. Kicking off the covers, he rose from bed and tugged a UT Austin T-shirt on over his pinstriped pajama pants. Then he made his way downstairs to the kitchen. Maybe a beer would help him sleep.

His house was only about a quarter size of the main house, but it still had plenty of room. Like the others, his mother had hired a professional to decorate the place, and Roth hadn't seen any reason to change a thing since his parents' deaths. The color scheme throughout was pale earth tones with splashes of turquoise and terracotta to give it a Western feel. And the masculine furniture in every room suited him. He remembered his mother telling him how after he married, he and his wife could make whatever changes they wanted. Marlene had probably expected that, by now, there would be a lot of feminine touches throughout the place, and that at least two of the four bedrooms would boast cribs and bunk beds as their centerpieces instead of the generic guest room and home office stuff they actually held.

The kitchen, especially, she'd probably assumed, would be cluttered with small appliances, colorful cookware and whimsical dish towels, with scribbled crayon drawings on the fridge. Instead, the only appliances he owned or used were the microwave and coffee maker. The cookware never left the cabinet, and there were no dish towels, since everything went straight into the dishwasher. The only thing magnetted to the fridge were the takeout menus for a half dozen local eateries. A family abode this house was not.

Sorry, Mom, he thought as he opened the fridge to find it filled with nothing but a few IPAs, a half carton of OJ, some of Kelsey's leftover spaghetti and a quartet of condiments that were probably all past their best-by dates. He reached for one of the bottles of beer and twisted off the cap with a satisfying hiss, made a mental note to at least buy some bacon or eggs or something and closed the fridge door.

When he turned around and looked at the empty kitchen again, he tried to envision it the way his mom and dad would have liked to have seen it—he and his would-be wife cooking up something at the stove while their two or three kids sat at the breakfast bar wanting to know if they could have a cookie while they waited for dinner to get done. A golden retriever named Daisy patiently awaiting a taste of whatever was on the countertop and an orange tabby named Milo sitting in the window, yelling at the squirrels who kept raiding the bird feeder on the other side. Disney tunes playing on the stereo and toys scattered about. A happy mess, his mother used to call the Fortune kitchen when it looked like that when they were kids.

Roth tried, but every time he tried to cement the vision it changed into a different one. What he imagined instead—more easily than he probably should have— was Antonia at the table pouring Cheerios onto a high chair where Georgie was cooing and laughing while he dry-rubbed some ribs he was about to carry out to the grill. Yeah. That thought had come way too clearly for his comfort.

He banished the image as soon as it materialized. No way should he be thinking about that. Even without all the emotional baggage he was juggling now, his lifestyle kept him way too busy to even think about starting a family. He didn't want to be a family man, anyway. He'd be a distracted husband and an absent father—which Antonia and Georgie especially didn't deserve. And besides, she was nowhere near ready to get involved romantically with anyone. The last thing either of them needed was to get involved with one another. The only reason he was thinking such bizarre thoughts in the middle of the night was because he was sleep-deprived—that was all.

But sleep, he knew, wouldn't come anytime soon, so he headed out to the patio to enjoy his beer and the balmy night. Too often, August in Texas was an unpleasant stew of heat and humidity, but they'd been lucky so far to be enjoying halfway-decent weather this year. The sky was mostly clear, a million stars scattered across it, but the moon had ducked behind some wispy clouds. Anything that had been stirring before was quiet now, no chirping crickets, no hooting owls, not even the hint of a breeze. And—

And there seemed to be a light on in the boathouse. Roth saw it just as he was about to take a seat in one of four Adirondack chairs positioned to give the sitter a spectacular view of the river. He stopped and moved to his left, to see the building more clearly. Yep. Definitely a light on down there. He was making a mental note to remind himself to turn it off in the morning when he realized the reason it was on was because someone was inside the boathouse. He saw a figure move back and forth in front of a window but couldn't tell who it was from this distance.

"What the…?" he murmured under his breath. He set his beer on a table beside the chair and made his way down the steps and the path beyond it to investigate.

The boathouse had been built before any of the guest-houses, almost immediately after his parents bought the main house as newlyweds. Roth's father had had a love for old boats and a knack for revamping them, and he'd purchased what even then had been an old sailboat—a

Sparkman twenty-one-footer that had been in terrible shape. Mark Fortune had brought it lovingly back to life and named it *Miz Marlene* in honor of his new wife, and the couple had always taken it out together whenever they vacationed here. That said, they'd also taught all of their kids how to sail it as soon as they were old enough, in case, someday, they wanted to borrow it the same way they would a family car—to have fun with their friends or to woo a romantic interest.

After the kids came along, his father had done the boat refurbishing all over again with an old, gorgeous Chris-Craft cruiser more suited to a big family that he'd christened *Summer Fun*. Sander and Roth and Harris had all made it a point to keep the boats in good working order over the years. To this day, their hulls and decks gleamed like new, and their engines purred like the well-oiled machines they were. The boathouse holding them sat on the river's edge, and, as was always the case with his parents, had been outfitted to the nines. There was a mini-kitchen and bathroom, a changing room with cushioned seating, and outdoor showers. Two long docks stretched out over the water that had doubled as a diving platform for the children.

They'd always called it the party house when Roth and his siblings were kids. But there hadn't been much partying going on here for a while.

As he drew nearer to the boathouse, Roth's suspicions were proven correct when he heard someone inside moving things around. Not frantically, as if they were rifling through the place looking for something to steal, but methodically, as if they were searching for something they'd lost. When he rounded the corner, he saw that the door was wide open, the yellow light from inside spilling into an irregular rectangle onto the dock. He stepped through and saw Sander inside, hands on hips, gazing up at the rafters. He looked like he'd dragged himself out of bed, too, because he was wearing gray sweatpants and a Dallas Mavericks T-shirt, and his dark blond hair was as untidy as Roth had ever seen it.

"Sander?" he said by way of a greeting.

His uncle turned with a start, but when he saw his nephew in the door, he relaxed. "You couldn't sleep, either?" he asked.

Roth shook his head. "What's got you up so late?"

Sander turned around to face him. "What *doesn't* have me up late these days?" he said with a weary sigh. "What's your excuse?"

Although Roth knew the answer to that full well— he still couldn't quite shake the image of Antonia and Georgie in his kitchen—he replied evasively, "Same as yours."

"I hate lying in bed awake," Sander muttered. "It's such a waste of time. So I thought I'd come down here and poke around to see if I could find the surprise your folks hid for you kids. I don't know if anyone's really had a good look around here in the boathouse yet."

"I think Harris and Zara did one day last summer," Roth said. He smiled. "But then I think they gave up pretty quick and took the day-sailer out instead. It was a nice day if memory serves."

Sander looked at the boat in question. "Your dad did know boats," he said, his voice traced with a tone that was a mix of wistfulness and good-natured envy. "He got that from our grandfather. Me, I ended up with the architecture gene from Mamaw's side of the family instead."

And Sander was an excellent architect at that, specializing in ranches both built from scratch and redesigned from old heaps. He'd been a late-life surprise to his parents, which was why he'd been so much younger than Roth's father. Sander had idolized Mark from an early age, though, from what Roth had been told, following around his big brother wherever he went, Mark mock-tolerating him when, really, he had loved his kid brother just as much.

"You want to come back to the house for a beer?" Roth asked. "I was just about to have one myself."

Sander took one last look around the boathouse, then nodded. "I'm not really paying as much attention to this search as I should be anyway. We should probably all sit down one day and organize a thorough search the way archaeologists do—make a grid and go square by square until we find the dang thing. Whatever it is."

They switched off the lights, locked up the boathouse, then made their way back to Roth's patio. Sander took a seat in one of the other chairs as Roth retrieved another IPA from the fridge and went back to his own. Then the two men clinked their bottles together, settled back in their chairs and looked out at the dark river.

After a moment, Sander said, "Your folks sure knew what they were doing when they bought this place. It's like a little slice of heaven."

Roth couldn't disagree. "I wish I could spend more

time here. I'm sure we all do. It's just so tough to get away from life sometimes."

"Well, we're spending time here now. I just wish it was under better circumstances. Not just Linc, but I can't believe it's been twenty years since your parents—"

Yeah. Roth couldn't believe it, either. There had honestly been times this month when he'd awoken in the morning and thought, for just the tiniest, merest nanosecond, that he was a kid again, and that the day ahead would be filled with running and swimming and rafting. And that he'd run home at the end of it all to find his mom in the kitchen taking fresh-baked cookies out of the oven while his dad carried a platter of hamburger patties and hot dogs out to the grill. Those summer days here in Emerald Ridge had been the best days of his life. Nothing he'd done as an adult even came close. Not the world travel, not the millions of dollars made, not the high-rise in the heart of Dallas. Nothing. He would give anything if he could turn back the clock and have one more day with his parents here in Emerald Ridge.

He tipped back his beer and swallowed, then looked at his uncle. Sander might be over forty now, but he hadn't changed a lot since he'd shouldered the mantle of guardian to a bunch of grieving kids at the age of twenty-four. There was silver threading his hair now, and a few lines around his eyes that gave him the look of a life well lived. But he was fit and good-looking, a man living his life with his own rules and on his own terms. That hadn't been the case twenty years ago, though, when Sander had given up everything to make sure the Fortune family stayed intact.

Roth looked back out at the river, striped with moonlight, lapping softly at the shore. His voice was even softer when he said, "I don't know if any of us ever properly thanked you, Sander, for taking us all in after Mom and Dad died."

He felt more than saw Sander turn in his chair to look at him. But his uncle said nothing.

"So let me say it now," Roth told him. "Thank you. Thank you for taking us all in and making sure we didn't get separated. Thank you for putting your life on hold for years for a bunch of confused kids. Thanks for listening to us when we needed to talk. Thanks for coming to all our games and recitals and everything else. Thanks for making sure none of us did anything stupid. Well, not *too* stupid," he amended with a chuckle. "And most of all? Thanks for being a mother and father both to us after we lost ours."

Roth did turn to look at Sander then, and found his uncle staring back at him hard. Not hard like he was angry. But like he was trying not to show how moved he was by Roth's words. He probably would have been better off trying to look angry. 'Cause he failed miserably trying to hide how deeply what Roth said had affected him.

Sander, too, turned to look at the river when he finally replied. "You don't have to tell me thanks," he said thickly. "You kids have shown me time and again over the years how much you appreciated it. And I learned a lot from all of y'all. But you're welcome," he finished, turning to look at Roth again, a genuine smile playing about his mouth. "It was a labor of love."

Roth smiled back. "Probably more like a labor of Hercules."

"Only sometimes," Sander assured him.

They sat in comfortable silence for another moment before Roth asked his uncle, "So have you developed any theories about Linc?"

Sander shook his head. "Not really. I still can't imagine what he must've gotten into that got him killed."

"Could've just been some random act of violence." Though Roth didn't really think that was likely. Not in a place like Emerald Ridge.

"Nah," Sander said. "An act of violence for sure, but I can't believe there was anything random about it. There has to be a reason for how Linc ended up the way he did. I just can't imagine what it would be." He drew another long sip of beer then swallowed. "For now, we're just going to have to let the local authorities do their thing. They'll have access to more information and more people than we do. I'm confident they'll figure this thing out before long."

Roth hoped so. Not only did he want justice for Linc, but he really couldn't leave his life on hold like this forever. He needed to get back to Dallas ASAP. He had things to do. People to meet. Work to take care of. Life to live. Yeah, he couldn't wait to get back to all that stuff. All that super important stuff. The sooner the better.

Anything to take his mind off of kissing Antonia Leonetti on her front porch, in the lavender twilight of nightfall, while fireflies glittered around them like fairies.

* * *

The week following Georgie's birthday party was, somehow, the most miserable one Roth could remember in his adult life. The previously pleasant weather took a turn for the worse, pummeling Emerald Ridge with one summer storm after another, until the whole place was a soggy, muddy, humid mess. Not only did it prevent any of the Fortunes from enjoying the very things they visited Emerald Ridge for, but it hindered the family's search for Mark and Marlene's surprise. Roth did his best to take advantage of being trapped in his house to catch up on the backlog of work at Fortune Capital that had built up since the beginning of the month. But even getting caught up with his overdue obligations, something that would normally make him feel productive and content with a job well done, he only felt more dissatisfied and irritable.

Worst of all, though, was that Roth had had to go back to Dallas *again* to see to a problem, and spend the night *again* in his too quiet, too empty condo. Then, upon returning to Emerald Ridge, he discovered that not only was the weather still crappy, there had there been no progress in Linc's murder case. In fact, the Emerald Ridge PD were more mystified than ever. Every new clue they uncovered had either resulted in a dead end or opened up a whole new avenue of investigation that was going to require more time and manpower.

By the time Friday night rolled around, the weather had finally cleared, but all of the Fortunes were feeling grumpy and frustrated, and their conversations over family dinner at the main house reflected that.

Why hadn't there been any breaks in Linc's case? Why couldn't they find a trace of whatever it was their parents had hidden? How much longer was this "long weekend" going to last? And how, dammit, were they going to manage if went on much longer?

Where it wasn't unusual for the family to spend the evening after dinner lounging around visiting, on Friday night, it was like they couldn't scatter quickly enough. As Priscilla and Zara returned to their houses, Sander said something about working on a new project upstairs while Kelsey took off to meet some friends in town. It was Roth's turn to share cleanup with his brother, Harris, and both men sped through the task with barely an exchange of a dozen words. It wasn't that any of them were mad at each other. It was just that they were all so disheartened by the lack of forward movement in…oh, everything…that they all just wanted to be left alone.

Roth was no exception. As he walked back to his house after pushing the button on the dishwasher and telling his brother goodbye, he felt like one of the week's dark rain clouds was following behind him, just waiting to open up again and douse him. It really had been a crummy week, both here and in Dallas. Dallas was starting to feel completely alien to him, but Emerald Ridge was starting to feel off, too. It was like neither of the places he'd always considered home felt like home anymore.

And he couldn't for the life of him understand why.

Virtually every moment he'd lived, virtually every memory he had, virtually everything he was…pretty much all of it was in one of those two places. The sensation that he suddenly didn't feel like he belonged in either one of them was just plain weird. What the hell had come over him to feel this way? Like he was going to have to find some whole new place to call home and start all over again. But where that place might be, or what he'd have to do to feel comfortable there, he couldn't imagine. Texas was *home*. Period. As was the Fortune family. So why, suddenly, did neither of those things feel like they were enough?

Still stewing, he strode up the driveway to his house, then climbed the porch stairs. He was about to turn the knob on the front door, but a creak from the swing at the other end of the porch made him look that way instead. Sitting in the middle of it was Antonia, looking like a clear summer sky in a pale blue sleeveless dress with her sun-kissed honey-brown hair falling over one shoulder. And just like that, the dark cloud that had followed Roth home evaporated.

Had it only been a week since he'd seen her? It felt like a lifetime had passed since that night on her own front porch. When they'd shared a kiss. Which they'd agreed was a mistake and that they'd vowed would never happen again. What was she doing here now? And how had she gotten here? He glanced over his shoulder to see her car parked in his driveway. He'd been so lost in thought, he hadn't even noticed it.

"Hey," he greeted her.

"Hey, yourself," she replied.

Then she smiled. And somehow, suddenly, Roth truly did feel as if he'd come home. He pushed the thought away. Antonia Leonetti was *not* his home. She was his business rival. It was just good to have a distraction, that was all.

"What are you doing here?" he asked lightly.

"Waiting for you. You forgot something when you left after Georgie's birthday party last week. I stopped by the other day, but there was no one home." She grinned again. "Then I ran into Zara in town yesterday morning, and she said you'd be back by tonight because it was your turn to clean up the kitchen after dinner. And if you weren't back before then, she was going to drive to Dallas and bring you back herself, because she's fed up with picking up the slack for you this week. So FYI and all that."

Roth chuckled. Yeah, that sounded like Zara. Then he remembered what it was he'd left at Antonia's house: the latest proposal the Leonettis had put together to buy Fortune's Vintages. He was about to tell her she'd made the trip to his place tonight for nothing when she held up a gift bag decorated with cartoon cowboys and cowgirls lassoing baby cows. He recognized it as one of the goody bags she'd sent home with all the other party guests last week. Roth had peeked inside one when they were lined up on a table outside, to see that they were filled with toys and trinkets and treats that were perfect for the under-ten crowd. Not exactly the kind of thing an adult would need. Even if one of the treats had been Goldfish crackers, his favorite when he was a kid.

"Thanks," he told her, "but I think I have enough Ring Pops and bubble wands for now. Save it for Georgie as a souvenir."

She stood, her gauzy dress flowing down to nearly

her ankles. "Oh, come on. There's a lot more to this goody bag than a Ring Pop and a bubble wand. There's also some Play-Doh, some M&M's, and a gen-one Pokémon. Gyrados."

Well, hell. Gyrados had been one of his favorite Pokémon when he was a kid.

"Oh, wait," she added, "there was something else in there, too, that just now fell out."

She looked behind herself and reached for something on the swing cushion. A dark blue folder. What a surprise. Strangely, though, even its appearance didn't make a dent in Roth's new and improved mood.

"I'll keep the Gyrados," he told her with a smile, "and the M&M's. The rest you can take back home. Including that damned folder."

"But you haven't even read the proposal."

"I don't need to read the proposal. I'm not selling Fortune's Vintages."

This time, she was the one to smile. "What if, this time, we're offering you a million billion trillion dollars? *And* a pony?"

He laughed.

"It could happen," she assured him.

"Fine," he told her. "For a pony, I'll look at it. But unless it's a painted pony, don't get your hopes up."

She laughed, too, then crossed the porch to give both the folder and goody bag to him. Instead of taking them from her, Roth asked, "Have you had dinner?"

She shook her head. "I came over here straight from a meeting with Leo and Gia and Bella. I figured you'd be home soon, so I've just been catching up with email on my phone while I waited."

"Where's Georgie?" he asked.

"With Bella and her kids. My niece and nephew love to play big brother and sister to their baby cousin. I wouldn't be surprised if I get a text later from one of them asking if Georgie can spend the night in their wing of the house with them because it's Friday, and they want to stay up late to make cupcakes and watch *Toy Story*. 'Oh, please please *please*, Aunt Antonia, puh-leeze.'"

As if cued by the comment, her phone dinged, and, after reading the text, she laughed again. Then she turned it so that Roth could see the screen. There was a message from her niece written almost verbatim to Antonia's comments. Except that they wanted to make snickerdoodles and watch *Finding Nemo*.

She immediately began to text back. "Normally," she said as she was typing, "I'd say no, because of Georgie's nighttime wakings. But for some reason she never has them after spending time with her cousins. Last week excluded," she quickly clarified when Roth was about to mention Georgie's distress the night of the party. "But I'm confident that night was only because she was over-stimulated from the festivities. It never happened before or since when she's been with the kids."

She finished typing, hit Send and looked at Roth. "Wow. I have a whole Friday night to myself."

"Then why don't I fix you some dinner?" he suggested.

Even though he'd just finished his own dinner half an hour ago. He had at least made a trip into town since that night last weekend, after inspecting his empty fridge, to pick up a few things at ER Grocery. He still wasn't sure why. Probably for the same reason he'd started entertaining ideas about adopting a dog and a cat and setting up a bird feeder outside. Whatever the hell that reason was.

At the moment, he didn't care. He just wanted to be with Antonia. Not for a romantic evening or anything like that, since they'd both made it abundantly clear there was no chance of that happening, what with her on the rebound and him being too busy and pragmatic and ruthless and cutthroat and…and…and all that other stuff he'd assured Priscilla he was that morning at Emerald Ridge Café. He couldn't remember now. Besides, it would be impolite to send Antonia home on an empty stomach. His mother would never forgive him for being so inconsiderate. That was all there was to it.

He pushed the door open and gestured for her to precede him into the house. It was as silent as a tomb, as always, but somehow, it didn't feel quite as lonely as it usually did. Antonia dropped both the gift bag and the proposal on the foyer table as she passed it, then strode into the living room that had always seemed so impersonal to Roth before, but suddenly didn't anymore. When she turned around to look at him, he realized she had no idea where the kitchen was—Why would he have thought she knew where the kitchen was?—so he strode past her with a gesture in that direction. She followed, and he told her to take a seat at the breakfast bar where he'd tried to picture his imaginary children the weekend before. He liked the reality of Antonia sitting there much better.

"What are you in the mood for?" he asked as he opened the fridge door. "I have sandwich stuff, sandwich stuff, and sandwich stuff. And also some sandwich stuff."

"Hmm... Do you have anything for sandwiches?" she asked with a grin.

Roth grinned back. "You're in luck. Coming right up."

He made short work of a couple of sandwiches for them, then opened a bottle of the Fortune's Vintages Malbec he'd brought from home. As he picked at his own second dinner—telling Antonia he'd probably just save it for lunch tomorrow, since he didn't really have much of an appetite for some reason—they chatted about the recently lousy weather and the lack of development in Linc's murder investigation. But where the same conversation with his family had been sullen and unproductive, talking about the same things with Antonia was lively and engaging. She had some interesting considerations about what might have happened to Linc. Had he had any visitors from out of town? What ever happened to that guy he didn't get along with in high school? And what about his messy breakup with that girl from El Paso who had been in town one summer?

"All good questions," Roth said as their inquisition wound down. "But none really have any concrete answers. At least none that the cops are sharing."

"I hope they know more than they're letting on," Antonia agreed. "Otherwise, this could go on for a long time."

And Roth wouldn't be leaving Emerald Ridge until

it was done. All the Fortunes had promised to stay until they found out what happened to Linc, in case any of them could be of help to the investigation. It might take some time but they would eventually find out what happened to Linc. Someone in Emerald Ridge had to know something that was going to blow the case wide open once it came out. He just hoped it was soon.

He looked at Antonia, who looked back at him. Though for some reason, at the moment, if he had to stay in town a little longer than originally planned, he kind of wouldn't mind.

Chapter Nine

By the time Antonia and Roth cleaned up their dinner, a soft drizzle had begun to fall outside. She told herself it was a sign that it was time for her to go home. She hadn't planned on staying this long at his place. She really had just intended to drop off the proposal he'd left at her house last week. Which, okay, she could have couriered the way she'd told him she would, but for some reason hadn't. Between the terrible weather and some disruptions at work, she hadn't been able to get away until the other day, when she discovered he wasn't home. She still had no excuse to stay any longer tonight. Other than that she was just having a nice time, talking to Roth.

"Well, I was going to suggest we sit outside for a bit," he said now, "and enjoy the first nice evening we've had for a while, but it looks like the night has other ideas."

"I should probably be going anyway," Antonia told him.

He glanced over at the opened bottle of wine. "But we haven't finished the Malbec," he murmured.

And it was a really good Malbec, too, she had to admit. Maybe even better than the one the Leonettis vinted themselves. Not that she would tell him that. Or Bella, for that matter, even if her sister deserved to know she had some competition in that regard. Maybe Antonia really should have one more glass, though, just to be sure.

"Oh, okay," she conceded. "Twist my arm."

Roth poured them each another glass, then nodded toward the living room. "There's still a nice view of the river from in there," he told her. "Not as nice as outside, but still good."

It had been daylight out when they came inside, so Roth hadn't turned on any lamps in the living room as they passed through it. He reached for one as they came in, then stopped himself when he must have realized how dark it was outside and how a light would just reflect in the glass of the open windows and mess up the view. The hills rolled softly away on the other side of the river, and the moon spilled a watery trail across its dark water. Wispy clouds wrapped the sky in a milky gauze, and a few stars winked back at them from behind it. The curtains fluttered softly in the breeze, the wind ruffling the trees while the rain pattered softly on the patio. If Antonia were a more whimsical woman, she would have said the night music outside was downright bewitching.

Roth's parents had chosen wisely when they bought this property, she thought. As beautiful as Leonetti Vineyards was, and as much as she loved sitting outside and admiring the deep greens and reds of the grapes, there was a lot to be said for a water view.

"Hydrotherapy," Roth said from beside her, his gaze

following hers. "That's what my dad used to call coming to Emerald Ridge. He could spend hours just sitting outside, looking at the water. And he loved taking out one of the boats."

"He wasn't wrong," Antonia said. "I might have to talk to Leo and Bella and Gia about us chipping in to buy a boat. I'm surprised Papa never bought one."

"I'll take you out on the sailboat next time you have a free day."

She was about to tell him she was free tomorrow but stopped herself. Number one, she wasn't free tomorrow, since she would be reclaiming her daughter from her niblings before lunch. For another...

Well, she knew there must be another reason she couldn't go out with Roth tomorrow. Or any other day. Oh, wait. Now she remembered. Because she was rebounding from the second stupid mistake she'd made with a man in less than two years. The last thing she needed was to make a third one. Three strikes, and she was *out*. Roth seemed like a good guy. But she'd thought Silvio and Charles were both good guys, too. Her judgment when it came to men was obviously a tad lacking, so she was going to have to make sure the jury stayed out on Roth Fortune for a while. It would be a long time before Antonia could even *think* about doing anything with a man. Other than trying to buy his vineyard, she meant.

They settled onto the sofa in the dark room, their gazes still fixed on the closing of the day outside. Even though it wasn't unusual for Georgie to spend the night with her cousins—or her grandmother, for that matter—it felt strange to Antonia to not to be going about her regular nighttime routine with her daughter. She'd all but forgotten what her evening rituals had been before becoming a mother. Something about enjoying quiet time and having a glass of wine after a meal—which, okay, check, she was doing that. Something about reflecting on life, the universe and whatnot. She'd done some of that tonight, too, so check. Something about making plans for the next day and the next week and the next year. Yeah, that one was going to have to wait. At least the bit about weeks and years. It was going to be one day at a time for her for a while. At least until she could trust herself to think straight again.

Then she looked at Roth and remembered other things she'd done in the evening pre-motherhood. Like spending time with a significant other. And even if those SOs had ultimately turned out to be SOBs, there had been a lot of nice evenings with them before that.

Antonia knew there were a lot of people out there who reveled in their singleness and in living—and being—alone. And, hey, more power to them. But she'd never been one of them. She liked the company of another human being in her life. And yes, Georgie definitely provided that, but conversations and activities with a baby were a tad limited. Antonia missed the company of another adult who wasn't an immediate family member. Even though only a couple of weeks had passed since her breakup with Charles, she already missed being part of a couple. Clearly, this taking time to figure things out wasn't going to be as easy as she'd hoped.

"Or we could take out the cruiser," Roth added, "if sailing's not your thing."

She realized then that she'd never replied to his offer one way or another. When she glanced over at him, he looked as if he were worried he might have offended her. In fact, nothing could have been further from the truth. Antonia would have loved to go out on the river with Roth. There was no way, though, that she could let herself do that. Not when she should be—had to be— keeping her distance from him. After tonight, she meant. Since there was almost no distance between them on the sofa. How had that happened?

So she told him evasively, "That sounds nice."

And it did sound nice. She just couldn't allow it to happen.

Roth looked as if he wanted to pin her down on a more specific answer, but he thankfully backed off and changed the subject. "I think if my folks had had their druthers, they would have lived full-time here in Emerald Ridge instead of Dallas."

"I don't blame them," she said. "I loved growing up here and can't imagine living anywhere else. It's the perfect place to raise Georgie."

Roth said nothing for a moment, only looked thoughtful. Then he replied, "Yeah, it is. I mean, Dallas is a great city, but..."

"But what?"

He shook his head. "I don't know. I love it there, too. It's just..."

"What?" she asked again.

Once again, he shook his head. "I don't know. I've

had to make a couple trips back since we all got to Emerald Ridge, and Dallas just feels a little...different... lately. I guess I just never paid attention to all the traffic and people and noise. Sometimes you look up and you can barely see the sky. But I do love the city," he hurried to assure her. Or maybe assure himself, she couldn't help thinking. "And it is by far the best place to run Fortune Capital. Right in the thick of things."

"And you have a lot of history there," she said softly.

"I do," he agreed. He looked at her again. "But I have a lot of history here, too."

For a long moment, they only gazed at each other and said nothing. Not that there was anything, really, to say. They'd both just voiced even more reasons why Antonia shouldn't be entertaining any silly ideas about starting something with Roth. As much as she wished— really, really wished—that she could. They both came from different worlds and would return to those worlds once his family's stay in Emerald Ridge came to an end. Roth was a businessman whose business was elsewhere. Antonia was a single mom who wanted her daughter to have as idyllic a childhood as she'd had herself. In CFO language, that was what was known as *the bottom line*. There could be no negotiating after that.

But I have a lot of history here, too.

His words echoed in her ears in a way that made her heart thump hard in her chest. The way he was looking at her made her pulse leap even faster. Because there was something in the way he said those words, and there was something in his eyes just then, eyes that seemed to open straight into his soul, that made her feel as if maybe, possibly, perhaps there was hope for the two of them after all. She just felt so good whenever she was with Roth. Things felt so right whenever she was with him. She tried to tell herself she was making excuses, that things had felt good and right with Silvio and Charles, too. Now, of course, she realized things hadn't been okay with them. Not the way they were with Roth. Because the way she felt with Roth was completely different from the way she'd felt with them. Roth was completely different from them, too.

Just as she had that night on her porch, when she had been too exhausted to think about what she was doing, she leaned in and brushed a kiss against his cheek, his skin warm and rough beneath her lips. She didn't know why she did it. It just felt like the thing to do. Antonia supposed she could blame the wine. But she'd grown up around wine. She'd been drinking it since she was thirteen, the age when her parents started letting each of their children have half a glass on special occasions. She knew how to pace herself with alcohol. Knew when she'd had too much. What she was feeling now had nothing to do with wine and everything to do with Roth. She missed the companionship, the intimacy, *the touch* of another human being. No. What she missed was the touch of Roth.

There was just something about this man that called to her on an elemental level.

So she moved her mouth to his, covering it in a kiss she meant to be soft and chaste and quick. Just to be companionable for a moment. Just to be close for a moment. Just to touch another human being, to touch Roth, for a moment. The moment they connected, however, Antonia felt anything but soft or chaste or quick.

Roth obviously didn't, either, because he kissed her back in a way that sent heat sizzling through her entire body. Then he roped his arm around her waist, hauled her into his lap and seized control of the embrace. When she gasped softly, he took advantage to escalate the kiss, tasting her deeply. When she wrapped her arms around his neck and pressed her body into his, he moved his other hand to her rib cage, cradling her breast in the V of his thumb and forefinger. Antonia splayed her hand open wide over the middle of his chest, and when she felt his own heart pumping frantically beneath her fingertips, she knew there would be no going back. She didn't want to go back. Not yet. Maybe not ever. She just wanted, for once, to stop thinking and be in the moment and just *feel*.

Roth was here with her in this moment. He was handsome. He was kind. He was sexy. The thrill rushing through her was something she couldn't ever recall feeling for her ex-husband or her ex-fiancé. What Roth made her feel was like nothing she could have ever imagined. So what else could she do but respond to it? And when his mouth moved from her mouth to her neck, when he urged his hand upward to completely cover her breast, what she felt was…oh. Oh, oh, *oh*. So good. So much better than anything she'd felt before. And it had been so long since she'd felt like this with anyone. So long…

She stopped thinking after that and lost herself to what was happening. Roth reached for the top button of her dress, while she freed the top button of his shirt. One button, two, three, four, until his shirt fell open completely and she could feel the cool kiss of the evening breeze skimming over her bared torso. She tugged his shirttail free, and he nudged one side of her dress down over her arm. As she undid the fastening at the waist of his jeans, he unhooked the front clasp of her bra. She cried out when he covered her breast with his mouth, and it was all she could do to draw down the zipper of his fly and tuck her hand inside. Her breath hitched in her throat when she found him hard and heavy beneath her palm, and she reveled at the twin sensations of mastering him and being mastered by him. At feeling both vulnerable and powerful in a way she never had before.

For long moments, they only explored each other, their hands and mouths wandering wherever they could, over jaws, necks, shoulders, torsos. Somehow, Antonia ended up on her back on the sofa with Roth atop her, her hips cradling his thighs, her hands tangled in his hair, her legs draped over the backs of his. He'd completely unbuttoned and opened her dress by now, so she pushed his shirt from his shoulders and skimmed her hands over the solid bumps of muscle on his back. Hot skin to hot skin was almost more than she could bear, and her breathing grew heavy and erratic.

He moved his mouth to her breast, laving her with the flat of his tongue, teasing her with its tip. Then he inched his hand between their bodies, down to the juncture of her thighs, stroking her over the damp fabric of her panties. She gasped again at the contact and reached for him once more, curling her fingers firmly around his shaft and stroking him up, then down, then up again.

Roth growled something incoherent under his breath, then moved their bodies again so that he was sitting on the sofa with her astride him.

Neither had said a word about the passion that had overtaken them out of nowhere, almost as if they'd both been afraid that speaking would somehow break the spell. Now Roth looked Antonia square in the eye, his eyes dark with wanting that she knew must be mirrored in her own.

And he asked roughly, "Are we really going to do this?"

She nodded, struggling to find her voice. Just as raggedly, she finally replied, "Yes. Yes, we are."

He grinned. She grinned back.

"Then we should probably take it into the bedroom," he told her. "I don't usually keep condoms on the coffee table."

Right. Safety first. Even if unsafe was the last thing she felt with Roth, she was glad one of them was thinking coherently. They rose from the couch, leaving his shirt and her dress behind, and he took her hand to lead her up the stairs to his bedroom. The house was dark and silent throughout, save the gentle patter of rain on the roof and windows. His bedroom was bathed in cloudy moonlight, giving it the appearance of something mystical and sublime. He turned down the bed, grabbed a condom from the nightstand, and then they were embracing again.

They kissed some more as they helped each other out of what little clothing they had left on, then they tumbled into bed to explore the parts of each other they hadn't gotten to yet. Roth rolled Antonia onto her belly and lay alongside her, pressing his lips to her shoulder blades before dragging soft butterfly kisses along the column of her spine and back up again. When she started to roll over to kiss him back, he stopped her midturn, until she was on her side facing away from him. Curving a hand over one hip, he moved against her, aligning his body with hers.

Then, before she realized what was happening, he was pushing one of her thighs forward to enter her from behind, slowly, deeply, completely. She groaned as he filled her, then purred when he moved his hand to her front, skimming it over her belly. As he thrust in and out behind her, he drove his fingers lower, burying them in the damp folds between her legs. All she could do then was grab the sheet in her fist and hang on, as one shudder of heat after another rocketed through her.

Roth seemed to sense when she was about to go over the edge, because he pulled out and rolled to his back, maneuvering her atop him. She settled on her knees above him, knowing she was the one in control this time. Slowly, she lowered herself over him, then rose again. Roth held her hips firmly and murmured something hot and erotic under his breath, then closed his eyes to enjoy the sensations rocking him. Over and over again, Antonia claimed him, until they were both nearing the edge. Once more, Roth moved their bodies again, so that she was on her back and they were facing each other. Then he kissed her as deeply as he entered her, until they were both crying out in their completion.

After that, they fell back onto the bed, still joined

together, gasping for breath and groping for coherent thought. But although Antonia did finally manage to catch her breath, thought was nowhere to be found in her brain. She could only *feel*. And what she felt was good. So good. In that moment, even if it was just for a moment, she felt better than she'd ever felt before. She just wished...

No. There could be no wishing when there was no thinking. And for now, there would be no talking, either. There was only feeling. Because everything was too perfect in that moment for anything else. She snuggled close to Roth. He draped a hand over her back and pulled her close, pressing a soft kiss against her temple. That simple gesture, too, made her feel good. And in that moment, even if just for a moment, that was the only thing she wanted in the world.

Antonia opened her eyes Saturday morning with way more clarity than she'd had when she closed them the night before. Too much clarity. Enough to know she should not be waking up Saturday morning in Roth's bed. Naked. With him lying beside her. Although it was early—barely a sliver of sunlight was visible over the rolling green hills out the window—she propped herself up on one elbow and gazed down at the man sleeping beside her. He lay on his belly, his bare back corded with muscle, his dark hair tousled lovingly by her own fingers. Roth had one arm tucked under his pillow and the other stretched out toward her, his fingertips just brushing her hip. More than anything, she wanted to bend down and drag soft butterfly kisses along his spine until he woke up. Woke up and then rolled over to make love to her again, with all the heat and urgency he'd shown the night before.

She still wished she could blame the wine for what had happened. But she couldn't. She knew exactly what she was doing when she kissed Roth last night. And when she wrapped her arms around him and pulled him closer. And when she made love to him. Twice. Her biggest problem now was that she didn't regret it as much as she knew she should.

But she did, unfortunately, regret it. As wonderful as it had been, it had been a mistake. A glorious, incredible, erotic mistake, but a mistake nonetheless.

Before she could stop herself, she moved her hand to trace her fingertip over the elegant curve of his muscled arm. Then across his shoulder and along the strong column of his nape. Roth stirred at her touch, his eyes fluttering open. He smiled when he saw her, rolled over onto his back, then wrapped an arm around her waist and pulled her down atop him. Before she could stop him— not that she really wanted to—he kissed her again, and she lost herself in the embrace for as long as she dared. But when she felt him swelling to life against her belly, and she realized how badly she wanted to welcome him inside her again, she made herself pull away. Then, tugging the sheet up around herself, she reluctantly scooted to the opposite side of the bed, as far away from him as she could.

Roth sat up, too, looking confused. "Everything okay?" he asked.

She nodded. "It's fine. I'm fine. Better than fine, really. You make me feel—"

She stopped herself before she said something else she was bound to regret. Something about how he made her feel complete. How he made her feel things she'd never felt before. How she wanted to keep feeling this way forever.

Those were all things she'd said to men before. Even if she realized now that she hadn't known what she was talking about when she did. She'd thought she'd been being honest with those men at those times. Now, of course, she knew better, because none of those men had made her feel the way Roth did. Even so, how could she be sure she knew what she was talking about now? She and Roth had spent one night together. And as incredible as it had been, there was no way to know how legitimate her feelings in that moment were after everything she'd been through.

She bit back a groan. Would she ever be able to trust her feelings again?

"I'm fine," she reiterated. But she said nothing more. Mostly because she didn't trust her words any more than she did her feelings.

"You sure?" he asked quietly.

She nodded.

He waited another beat, to see if she would elaborate, then told her, "It's early. We don't have to get up yet. We could, um, sleep in and have breakfast in town." When she still said nothing, still didn't even turn to look at him, he added, "Or we could go ahead and get up now, and I could fix us some breakfast. Pretty sure I have some bacon and eggs around here somewhere."

"That's okay," she told him. "I should probably be heading home."

He was silent for another telling beat. Then, very quietly, he said, "But you mentioned last night that you don't have to get Georgie until lunchtime."

"No, but..."

But what? she asked herself. *But I have to get myself as far away from you as I can so that I can think straight?* Yeah, that probably wasn't going to be the best thing to say at the moment. Then again, she should be honest with him, she told herself. As truthful as she could be, anyway. She owed him that.

She did pivot around to look at him then, snugging the sheet more tightly around herself. "Look, Roth, about last night..." She squeezed her eyes shut tight when she realized she was already turning what they'd shared together into a cliché. But hey, what she'd had with Charles had turned into a cliché. Her marriage to Silvio had been a cliché. Was that how she was going to end up living her life? Like some badly written stereotype?

She opened her eyes again and forced herself to meet Roth's gaze. "I'm sorry. Didn't mean to make it sound like a bad movie."

He grinned a little, but there was nothing happy in the gesture. She could tell he knew what was coming. Worse, she suspected he wasn't going to disagree with her.

"Last night shouldn't have happened," he finished

for her. "Just like the kiss last week shouldn't have happened."

She nodded. "Yeah. I'm not sure I'll go so far as to say we made a mistake, but..."

Mostly, she wouldn't go so far as that because it sounded rude. But deep inside, she knew it had been a mistake. And Roth, she was reasonably certain, felt the same way.

"It still shouldn't have happened," he finished for her again.

"I'm sorry I let things go too far."

"I'm not sorry at all," he immediately countered. "I think what happened last night was unavoidable. There's just been something—" here, he stopped to gesture between the two of them, as if there was some invisible force holding them together "—something between us that neither of us could resist. If last night didn't happen last night, it would have happened eventually."

He was right. Ever since that first day he'd approached her in town to tell her what he'd overheard Charles say, there had been something tugging at both of them. That first night he'd come to her house, when they'd spoken so frankly about their own botched romantic experiences, she was pretty sure he'd been as surprised by their camaraderie as she'd been herself. It had only grown that evening after Georgie's birthday party, when they'd shared that wonderful kiss. And it had grown more as they'd talked last night. Whatever the something was, it had been moving the two of them closer and closer to last night. They'd been physically attracted to each other from the start. Discovering they had a lot in common had taken that attraction to the next level.

Sometimes these things just happened. Maybe the reason for what drew them together was as simple as loneliness. Or maybe they'd both just needed the comfort of someone else in the aftermath of bad things that had occurred. For her, it had been breaking up with Charles. For Roth, it had been losing Linc Banning so tragically.

But loneliness and the need for comfort weren't things either of them should be building anything on. Maybe neither of them should be surprised that they'd turned to each other so intimately last night. But it wasn't wise to try to find something in their reaction to each other that was anything beyond superficial.

"I should go," she said again.

This time Roth didn't object. He only gazed at her in silence, looking as if he were giving himself the same kind of talking-to that she was. And not liking what he was hearing any more than she did. But knowing he was right. Like she was.

Without a word, they both rose from bed, turning their backs on each other to give themselves privacy while they put on what clothes had made it to the bedroom with them. Roth headed to the en suite bathroom, giving her the space and time she needed to return to the living room and gather up the rest of her things. By the time he returned, she had just finished buttoning up her dress, and he was clad in a pair of gray pajama pants and a black T-shirt.

"Let me at least fix us some coffee," he offered.

As much as she told herself to get out while the getting was good, she figured she probably shouldn't be operating any heavy machinery until she had some caffeine coursing through her system. So she nodded and thanked him, then followed him into the kitchen. The sun was still creeping up over the horizon, and the remnants of last night's drizzle still clung to the trees outside, making them shimmer like silk in the early dawn. She could easily get used to waking up in a place like this, with a man like Roth, every morning. Very, very easily.

No, she couldn't, she told herself. Even without all the complicated feelings, his life was in Dallas, and hers was here. He was wedded to his work. She was devoted to her daughter. If he went as far with Fortune's Vintages as he seemed to want to go, the two of them could be even more at odds professionally than they already were. No, maybe none of those things individually was an insurmountable obstacle. But together—and with who knew how many more differences that could creep up between them—it was just too much. And considering the way things had worked out for her in the past— and for Roth, too—it was reasonable to conclude that this thing between them, whatever it was, would at best fizzle out and at worst blow up in their faces.

They sipped their coffee mostly in silence, neither quite able to look at the other, then Roth walked her out to her car. The sun was fully up now, and the day stretched before them. Antonia had no idea how she would spend it once she collected Georgie from her cousins, but she was pretty sure her agenda included lots of regrets. She just wished...

She shook off the thought. If wishes were horses and all that. What wishes were was fantasy. Antonia needed to look at reality now. And the reality was that she needed to stop thinking about Roth and focus on herself. She had a lot of work to do there. It was going to be a long time before she trusted her feelings about... oh, everything.

"When do you have to go back to Dallas?" she asked him as she opened her car door. "For good, I mean?"

He blew out an exasperated sound and restlessly rubbed the back of his neck. "We're all staying in Emerald Ridge until Labor Day, at least. But even later than that if there haven't been any developments in Linc's case. We've all promised to stay here until we know who killed him. With any luck, that'll be before the end of the month."

She nodded. She wanted to ask him if he thought he'd be back any time after that. Then she reminded herself it didn't matter.

"I had a good time last night," she murmured softly.

He met her gaze and held it. "I did, too."

"Thank you for dinner. And coffee."

"Thank you for bringing by my goody bag. Those M&M's won't last long."

"And don't forget to look over the proposal." Pointedly, she added, "Leo is looking forward to your reply."

"Will do," he said in a way that told her he had no intention of doing that and would be sending her brother his decline of the offer as soon as she was out of sight.

She wanted to tell him she'd see him around. But she was pretty sure they both knew that, even if they did see each other around town, they wouldn't do more than wave or nod hello. What was the point? They were parting on good terms, but they were definitely parting.

"I hope things go well with Linc's investigation," she said.

"Thanks. And I hope Georgie works out whatever's going on with her."

"Me, too."

Another taut moment passed, with neither of them wanting to be the first one to say it.

Finally, Antonia told him, "Goodbye, Roth."

He took a step backward. "Goodbye, Antonia."

She folded herself into her car and pulled the door closed behind her. Then she started the engine and threw it into Reverse. She gave her full attention to backing out of the driveway and shifting into Drive, as if she were a sixteen-year-old learning for the first time how the different gears worked. Then, still looking forward, she lifted a hand in farewell and drove away.

In the rearview mirror, she saw Roth standing at the foot of his driveway, his hand lifted in the air much as hers was. Then he settled both hands on his hips. He kept watching her, though, until she turned off the access road to his house and onto the main drive of the Fortune compound. Then he was completely out of site.

As she turned onto the main road that would take her home, Antonia cursed herself for forgetting to take her sunglasses out of the glove compartment before she left. Because she was driving east, and the sun was so bright, it was starting to bring tears to her eyes.

Chapter Ten

Although the weather in Emerald Ridge improved enormously the last week of August, leaving the skies blue and sunny every day, Roth's mood only darkened. Despite the fact that things at Fortune Capital were going gangbusters, and even after he finally got caught up with his backlog of work, his temperament didn't improve.

Even Priscilla's discovery of a lockbox at the very back of their father's closet that they'd hoped for a brief, shining moment might be the missing surprise didn't make a dent in Roth's dejection. Especially after it ended up holding nothing but a couple of games his parents had confiscated one summer when they'd all gotten too preoccupied by them. And hell, he ought to be over the moon about being able to play *Assassin's Creed: Brotherhood* again. Harris and Kelsey sure were. By dinnertime with his family the final Saturday of August, the rest of the Fortunes were in excellent spirits, but Roth's own humor was sullen. He just felt lousy. About everything and everybody. And he had no idea why.

Okay, that wasn't entirely true. He did know why. He missed Antonia. But he also knew that the two of them separating had been the right thing to do. They'd had a nice couple of weeks together, but nothing was going to grow out of a nice couple of weeks. They called two different cities home. They lived two separate lifestyles. They had completely different priorities. They were at odds professionally. And on top of all that, Roth's focus for his entire adult life had been building and running a business—the kind of business that had always required, and would always require, constant supervision and attention. The center of Antonia's life, for the rest of her life, was going to be raising her daughter. As much as they liked each other, there was no way to join their lives—or themselves—together in any way that would work. Roth couldn't be part of a family, and Antonia needed someone who could and would make family their number one concern. There was just nothing in that mix that added up to a solid future together.

He knew it was just going to take time and that he needed to move on. And he *was* moving on. Or trying, at least. In a few months' time, he was sure to be back to normal again. He just needed to keep moving forward.

He just wasn't sure, exactly, what he was supposed to move forward to.

Ah, dammit. He'd figure it out, he assured himself as he joined his siblings and uncle and cousin on the patio of the main house after dinner. He'd been figuring things out for himself for more than a decade. Though he did kind of feel more lost at the moment than he'd ever felt before…

He heard more than listened to his family making easy banter and laughing about the prior week's events. But none of the revelry rubbed off on him. Even when

Harris suggested that they all stay home tonight and watch *Tombstone*, an obvious attempt to specifically improve Roth's mood, since they all knew that was his favorite movie, he only grumbled about having other plans. Not that he actually had other plans. He just didn't even want to do something fun with his family, because he was too busy being irritable.

"You have been so grumpy tonight," Priscilla chided him. "What's up with that?"

"He's been grumpy all week," Harris corrected her.

Sander agreed. "He didn't even want to go with me and Kelsey when we took out the sailboat the other day. When was the last time any of you ever saw him decline a day out on the water?"

"I've been busy," Roth reminded his family—grumpily, he couldn't help noticing.

"I'm sure it's completely unrelated," Priscilla piped up, "but I ran into Antonia Leonetti in town the other day, and she was in a terrible mood, too. Isn't that weird?"

Roth almost perked up at that. Almost. Just hearing Antonia's name made his pulse hitch a little faster. But he hated that she was feeling as lousy as he was. He guessed she needed time, too, to move on from what had happened between them and remind herself what a bad idea it would have been to continue with it.

He said nothing in response to Priscilla's comment. What was there for him to say?

Zara, however, seemed happy to chime in. "I heard little Georgie took her first step the other day."

Now Roth did look up. Georgie had taken her first

step? And he hadn't been there to see it? Then he gave himself a mental slap. Well, of course he hadn't been there to see it. Why would he feel like he should have been there in the first place? Antonia's daughter was her responsibility, not his. Still, he wished he could have seen it happen when it did.

"I bet that was adorable," Kelsey said. Like his two sisters, she had her attention fixed completely on Roth. As did Sander and Harris.

"Totally," Zara agreed. "I was talking to Gia Leonetti while we were waiting for our orders at Coffee Connection, and she told me how Georgie had been crawling around looking up at the furniture for the last month like she was about to grab it and haul herself to standing…"

This Roth knew, since he'd seen the little girl doing exactly that at her birthday party. Always with her mother or another Leonetti following close behind, filming with their phones, in case that was the day she decided to have a go at the standing-on-her-own-two-legs thing. But every time Georgie caught one of them watching her, she smiled and sat right back down on her booty as if to say, *Nope. Not ready yet.*

"And that she just up and went for it the other day," Zara continued. "She grabbed the sofa, yanked herself up and pulled herself along the whole length of it before sitting back down again."

Damn. Roth really would've liked to have seen that.

"I bet Antonia is delighted," Kelsey said.

"You'd think, wouldn't you?" Zara replied. "But Gia said that, as happy as she was in the moment, it didn't last. And that Antonia's been really down about something." Now Roth's sister looked at him again. As did everyone else. And she added meaningfully, "I can't imagine what."

How did they all know he and Antonia had been... doing stuff together that they shouldn't have been doing? They'd always been at either her house or his and hadn't once appeared in public as a couple. Of course, there had been more than one adult coming and going at Georgie's party, and a lot of the adults of Emerald Ridge did seem to include *gossipmongering* at the top of their daily to-do list, but still. He and Antonia hadn't even known themselves what was going on that day. Not until that evening, when they'd enjoyed that kiss on her front porch.

"Why are y'all looking at me?" he asked his family. "I didn't do anything to put Antonia in a bad mood."

Priscilla was opening her mouth to say something in response to his remark, but the front doorbell rang out, crisp and clear. All six Fortunes exchanged a curious look.

"Anybody expecting someone?" Sander asked.

They all shook their heads.

Sander turned to head back into the house, but Roth, closest to the door, raised a hand to stop him. "I'll get it."

He couldn't imagine who it could be when none of them was expecting anyone, but who he found on the other side was someone he wouldn't have guessed in a million years. Finn Morrison. Talk about a blast from the past. It felt like a million years since Roth had seen him. He'd been Zara's summertime boyfriend when they were teenagers. Maybe even her full-time boyfriend. Although Finn had never visited them in Dallas, Roth couldn't recall Zara ever really dating anyone else when they weren't visiting Emerald Ridge in the summers. Finn grew up here and had worked at the country club when they were kids, which was where he and Zara met. Last Roth had heard, if he was remembering correctly, the guy was doing something in the oil business.

One thing that was ingrained in his memory, though, was how Finn had broken Zara's heart back then. Even though a decade had passed, there were times when Roth suspected his sister still wasn't quite over it. There had been more than one family trip to Emerald Ridge over the years where Zara had opted out, often at the last minute and sometimes with excuses that bordered on the ridiculous. It was impossible for any of them to not suspect she was avoiding the place specifically because she didn't want to see her ex.

Come to think of it, Roth couldn't recall seeing Finn at all since the family had come to town a month ago, and he hadn't heard a word about him from anyone here. Hell, the Fortunes themselves hadn't talked about him in years. At least, Roth hadn't. Maybe Zara and Priscilla still did. He wished he could say Finn looked good, since that was generally the sort of generic compliment people paid to each other when they hadn't seen each other for a long time. Truth of the matter was, though, Finn didn't look good at all.

Roth suddenly flashed on a memory of fourteen-year-old Zara insisting her new fifteen-year-old boyfriend Finn was soooo handsome, he could have been the lead singer in a boy band. And how the rest of the family had ribbed her for the remainder of the summer, making up names for said fictional band. *NSTINK. Wrong Direction. New Kids Without Socks. And yeah, okay, the man Finn had grown into could probably still earn a decent living dancing on a stage in baggy pants and a headset. The clear blue eyes, the tousled blond hair, the scruffy jaw—all lent themselves to showbiz good looks. But Finn also looked tired. Really tired. Like he hadn't slept in a long time. And there was an edge of uneasiness in both his expression and his posture that was undeniable.

"Finn, hey," Roth greeted him. "Long time, no see."

The other man nodded. "Yeah, I'm in and out of Emerald Ridge on a fairly regular basis. Guess I've mostly missed you guys when you were here." He grinned, but that, too, seemed uneasy. "Sometimes I feel like I spend more time away than I do at home. I just got back into town this morning, as a matter of fact. I've been in the UAE for the last few weeks. Abu Dhabi."

Well, that explained the look of extreme fatigue. Flying from one side of the planet to the other could wreak havoc on a person. Still, he wasn't sure what else to say to a guy he hadn't seen or thought about for years, and who might not even be welcome at the house by at least one member of his family. What was Finn even doing here?

"So…how the hell are you?" he finally asked the other man.

He looked past Finn, at the late-model—and very expensive—sports car parked in the driveway that obviously belonged to him. Then he looked again at Finn, who was wearing what Roth recognized as the kind of clothing worn by men who could afford to spend a lot to look casual—bespoke Western shirt, hand-tooled cowboy boots and blue jeans that cost way too much to be sold in any department store. The man was obviously doing a lot better now than he had been when they were kids—at least financially.

Finn expelled a restless sound. "Not great, if you want to know the truth. Can I come in?"

Not sure it was a good idea, Roth hesitated.

Finn seemed to be neither surprised nor put off by his reluctance. "Look, I'm sorry to just show up here out of the blue like this, but I really need to talk to all of you." When Roth still didn't respond, he added, "It's about Linc Banning."

Roth remembered then that Finn and Linc had run in the same circles when they were teens, both coming from working class families but being surrounded by wealthy people thanks to their or their family's employment. But they'd never seemed to Roth like they were good friends. Though, really, Linc had kept his distance from almost everyone back then, even the Fortunes. Roth wondered if Finn and Linc had still run in the same circles as adults.

"I heard about his murder as soon as I got back into town," Finn continued, "and I got so much mixed information that I finally went to the police station to find out what was going on." After a tense pause, he added, "And I also kinda felt like I had to tell them about a weird interaction I had with Linc the week before he was…the week before he died. It's something you and your family should know, too, since there was a time when y'all and

Linc were pretty close. And I suspect y'all have probably been hearing a lot of contradicting stories, too."

He wasn't wrong. Seemed like everyone Roth had spoken to over the last few weeks had heard something different about Linc's behavior and whereabouts before his death, and they all seemed to have their own theories about what had led to his murder, few of them based on anything substantial.

At Finn's admission, Roth had no choice but to open the door wider and invite him inside. Anything he and his family could learn about Linc overshadowed any years-old hurt feelings that might or might not even still exist.

"Come on in," he said.

After another hesitation, Finn crossed the threshold, immediately driving his gaze around the room. When he saw that it was empty, he turned to Roth again. "Where is everybody?"

"Out back. We just finished dinner."

"Sorry to interrupt family time," Finn apologized. "I know how important that is."

Roth remembered Finn had lost both of his parents and never had any siblings. He wondered who the guy considered family these days.

"It's not an interruption," he assured him. "We've been in Emerald Ridge for almost a month. It's fine." He just hoped Zara would think it was fine, too. He jerked his head toward the kitchen and began to walk in that direction. "You want coffee?" he asked as they made their way. "Or there's still some wine."

"Coffee would be great," Finn said. "My body is

still getting used to the time change. My brain thinks I should just be waking up."

Roth chuckled as they entered the kitchen. Through the sliding doors, he saw the rest of the Fortunes out on the patio, enjoying what was left of the day. Sander was nursing a fire to life in the firepit while Priscilla coached him from behind. Harris was in one of the lounge chairs chatting with Kelsey, who was in the one beside it. Zara was apart from the others, at the edge of the patio, looking out over the grassy expanse of the yard to the tree line in the distance, where the sun was dipping low, staining the sky with a spectacular play of pink and yellow. It was going to be another gorgeous Texas sunset. As far as Roth had traveled—and he'd been around the world more times than he could count—he didn't think he'd ever seen a sunset as gorgeous as the ones they had in his home state.

He and Finn chatted about his flight as Roth poured him a cup of coffee, and Roth couldn't help noticing how Finn had spotted Zara outside already and had his gaze honed on her as the two of them headed to the sliding doors to join the others. When Roth pushed one open and stepped through, Sander and Priscilla looked up from the firepit to greet him. Whatever they were going to say, though, was cut short when Finn exited the house behind him, and neither said a word. Harris and Kelsey turned around to see what was going on, and they, too, stopped midconversation to gaze in astonishment at their guest. Only Zara, lost enough in thought to be oblivious to what was happening behind her, didn't react.

Not until Finn said, "Hey, everyone. Been a long time."

That was when Zara turned around with a start, and everyone stopped looking at Roth and Finn to look at her instead.

She didn't look too great, either, just then. Her mouth dropped open in faint surprise, and her dark blond brows arrowed downward. She looked like someone who'd just been pinched—hard. For a second, Roth thought she was going to bolt for the tree line she'd just been studying. But she rallied quickly, shooting each of her family members a reassuring smile. She didn't, however, say anything or move from where she was standing. Priscilla, though, seeming to detect something the others couldn't, rose immediately from her chair to place herself prominently between Zara and Finn, as if she were deliberately blocking his view of their sister. Or maybe blocking her sister's view of him. Then she covered the length of the patio to join the two men standing at the door.

"Wow, Finn Morrison," she said. "It really has been a long time."

Roth looked at Finn. Had he thought the guy looked bad before? 'Cause suddenly, he looked even worse. Like someone who was not just exhausted, but more than a little distressed, too.

"Good to see you, Priscilla," he replied. Then he craned his head around her to look at the others, greeting each by name. "Sander, Kelsey, Harris… Zara."

Roth looked at his other sister. Where his uncle, cousin and brother all murmured hellos, most of them sounding sincerely happy to see their guest, Zara only lifted a hand and gave Finn a half smile. The guy looked a little disappointed by the tepid response, but he cut right to the chase.

"I'm sorry to interrupt everyone's evening," he said again. "But I just got back into town today and heard about Linc Banning, and a few people said y'all stayed in town to keep track of the investigation. And I came here tonight because I thought you might be interested in hearing about something that happened between me and Linc the week before his death."

He finally stopped to take a breath, and all the Fortunes exchanged curious looks.

"What kind of something?" Roth asked.

"It was weird," Finn told them. "I was packing for a trip to the UAE, where I've been all month—my company was looking into a merger with an oil producer there—and I got a text from some number I didn't have in my contacts. It was after ten at night, and I couldn't imagine who would be texting me that late. Turned out to be Linc Banning, who I haven't even spoken to in years, telling me he wanted to get together the next day."

Roth furrowed his brow. "How'd he get your number if you guys haven't spoken for a while?"

"No idea," Finn replied. "I try to keep my private number private, but I guess you can find anybody these days if you try hard enough. I told him I wouldn't be able to see him because I was flying out late the next morning and wouldn't be back for a few weeks. So he asked if he could come over right then because he needed to talk to me. I told him whatever it was would have to wait, because I had a lot to do."

At this, for some reason, he looked at Zara, who, Roth hadn't been able to help noticing, had been studying Finn relentlessly since he started talking. The moment his gaze met hers, though, she turned her head to look at the fire crackling merrily in the firepit. Finn continued to look at her for a few seconds, then he, too, pulled his gaze away, back to the Fortunes surrounding him.

"Next thing I know," he continued, "there's a knock at my door, and it's Linc. The minute I opened it, he came in, talking a mile a minute. About how he'd gotten ahold of my adoption records and had them in a safe deposit box. And how those records would tell me everything I wanted to know about where I came from. And he told me he would sell them to me for a very fair price."

"*Sell* them to you?" Sander asked. "What the hell does that mean? Makes it sound like you were some kind of black-market baby. And where did he even get them in the first place?"

Finn shrugged. "I know. None of it makes sense. I mean, it's never been any secret that I was adopted. My parents told me about it as soon as I was old enough to understand, and it wasn't something I ever kept secret. But my mom and dad never gave me any details, even when I got older and wanted to learn more about my birth parents. They told me they had no idea and reassured me that *they* were my parents and said I should be happy with that. And I was happy with that," he hurried on. "I am happy with that. They were great parents."

"But now they're gone," Roth said, "so there's no

chance you'll ever be able to ask them any questions about any of this."

Finn nodded. "I mean, pretty much every kid who's adopted gets curious at some point about where they came from before the papers were signed. I was no different. I would have loved to know more about my beginnings. Hell, I'm still curious about it. Probably always will be."

"How did Linc get your adoption records?" Sander asked again. "Even lawsuits don't usually open those up if they were sealed from the beginning."

"He wouldn't tell me," Finn replied. "But the cops think it might have something to do with what happened earlier this year. That whole Courtney Wellington situation with the ranch sabotage that she orchestrated at the Fortune's Gold Ranch and Spa? I heard she spent months stealing their horses and raiding the property. And all that other stuff she was mixed up with?"

Even though the Fortunes had been back in Emerald Ridge for less than a month, all of them had heard the stories about Courtney. About how, at the beginning of the year, the rich widow had connived to take advantage of a former employee of the now-defunct Texas Royale Private Adoption Agency, an elderly woman who was frail and sick and possibly mentally diminished to boot. Courtney had heard the woman still had hard copies of a lot of the agency's adoption records and had offered her a pile of money to get her hands on one of those sealed files. The woman, in turn, had had a pile of medical bills so agreed to sell the adoptee's records to Courtney, probably not even realizing the severity—or potential illegality—of what she'd agreed to do.

"Man, that was some scandal," Harris recalled. "What everyone thought for decades was a legitimate adoption agency turned out to be nothing but a money-grabbing scam selling babies to the wealthy highest bidders. The agency even split up some multiple births."

Something all of the Fortunes knew, because one of the victims had been their cousin Drake, on the other side of the family tree. Drake, adopted as a baby, had had an identical twin he never knew about. Not until Courtney Wellington got ahold of Drake's adoption records and lured that twin, Cameron Waite, to town.

"Oh, jeez, don't tell us you have a secret twin, too," Kelsey burst out. "That would be awful."

Finn was shaking his head before she even finished the question. "I was a single," he said. "That much Linc did tell me."

"So do you think that he got the idea to sell your file to you from the news reports about Courtney buying Drake's adoption records from that former employee?" Sander asked.

"I don't know," Finn replied. "Maybe. But to be honest, I really can't wrap my brain around any of this. I always assumed my adoption went through the usual process, all legal and aboveboard. But even after talking to the police, I'm still not sure. I mean, my parents adopted me from Texas Royale, but it's not like they had a ton of money to pay for me. They were hardworking folks, but we never had anything but the necessities when I was growing up."

"Maybe that's why," Kelsey said. "Maybe they spent all their money to adopt you."

The comment seemed to hit Finn hard, but he recovered quickly. "Maybe. Now that Courtney's crimes have been exposed, the cops are looking into whether Linc possibly bought the files from the same ex-employee she approached. Took advantage of her the same way that awful Wellington woman did."

"Oh, no," Priscilla said. "This just gets worse and worse. What happened to Linc to turn him into the kind of person who could trade in emotional currency, selling people their own history? That's just…"

She shook her head before finishing. Probably, Roth thought, she couldn't think of a word bad enough to describe what Linc had been doing. He sure couldn't think of one himself.

"So it could be," Sander said, "that Linc had more than just your records."

"That's what the cops are thinking, too," Finn replied.

Priscilla looked stricken. "Was this how Linc was planning on getting rich? By selling adoptees hungry for knowledge about themselves the records that might give them answers? I can't believe he would prey on people that way."

"We don't know what his circumstances were like after his mother's death," Sander reminded her. "Things change. And sometimes they change for the worse. A lot of grieving people rise above that and turn adversity into prosperity. But some people get desperate and don't see any way out but the wrong way."

Each of the Fortunes shared a look. Roth figured everyone was probably thinking the same thing he was. How lucky they all were to have been born into the situation they had been, with loving parents who'd had the foresight—and the wealth—to make sure their children never wanted for anything. Just sheer dumb luck that their lives were going well when the lives of so many others weren't. Evidently Linc Banning included.

"So did you tell Linc you would buy your records from him?"

Surprisingly, the question came from Zara. It was the first thing she'd said since Finn's arrival, and he seemed genuinely relieved by her interest. Or maybe he was just grateful that she was speaking to him at all.

"I did," he said. He backtracked to where he had begun his story, with Linc showing up at his house with the offer to sell. "My flight wasn't leaving until late morning the following day, so we arranged to meet first thing in the morning for breakfast somewhere in town. I told him to text me the time and place and tell me how much cash to bring, since he kept dancing around an actual figure."

"What happened when you met him for breakfast?" Kelsey asked.

Finn shook his head. "We never met. I woke up to a text from him saying he changed his mind and didn't want to sell me my records. Then there was another text right after that saying he made a mistake and that he didn't even have my records at all."

Kelsey looked as confused as Roth felt. "Why would he contradict himself like that?" she said.

"Your guess is as good as mine," Finn told her. "People do crazy stuff sometimes, and I hadn't talked to him for years. I thought maybe he was in trouble and just grasping at straws, but when I got back into town and heard he'd been murdered..." His voice trailed off.

Roth finished for him, "You thought maybe he was in a lot more trouble than you realized."

Finn nodded. "That's when I went to the cops to share what happened between Linc and me."

"Did you hear anything new from the police that hasn't been made public?" Priscilla asked.

"Not really," Finn said. "Just that they think I'm probably not the only one Linc approached. They're staying tight-lipped otherwise. Understandable, I guess." He looked thoughtful for a moment. "But the upside to all this is that they have a whole new direction to take their investigation in now. They hadn't heard anything about the adoption stuff from anyone else. And since they believe there must be other folks out there that Linc tried selling information to, they said this is the kind of thing that could absolutely contribute to a motive for murder."

"Well, we know it's not Courtney," Priscilla said, "since she's parked in jail where she belongs. I'm sure the police are going to talk to her about this, but I can't see her cooperating since it could just incriminate her even more."

"What Linc was doing was almost like blackmail," Harris said. "Which doesn't jibe at all with the guy we knew."

The others nodded their agreement.

"Then again," he added, "none of us besides Priscilla has had any kind of contact with him since we were kids."

"It doesn't match up with the Linc I saw last month, either," Priscilla told them. "None of this makes any sense. But now I kinda maybe understand why he ghosted me after that one night we went out. He must have known what he was doing was wrong, and he didn't want to risk me finding out."

"Or," Zara said softly, "he didn't want to risk you getting involved and getting hurt. Which *does* jibe with the Linc we all knew."

Roth couldn't help thinking Zara was looking more at Finn when she said that than she was at Priscilla. Obviously, there was still something going on with Zara where her old boyfriend was concerned. Damned if Roth could figure out what it was, though.

"Anyway," Finn said, his tone indicating he was winding things down, "I figured you guys deserved to know what I told the police. Linc wasn't the most social guy in Emerald Ridge, but he always thought really highly of you Fortunes. You were the closest thing to a family the guy had."

In spite of everything he'd learned about Linc tonight, Roth was comforted by what Finn said. Maybe Linc had taken a wrong turn at some point in his life, but that had been his choice to make, and not because of anything terrible that happened to him as a kid. His mother had been a kind, sweet woman, and all of the Fortunes had done everything they could to include Linc in their lives and be both friend and family to him.

But there was still a lot up in the air. *Did* Linc have

Finn's adoption records at some point? Did someone maybe steal them from him? Was it the killer? If Linc did have the records, why did he renege on selling them to Finn? And what happened to all the other files the ex-employee of the adoption agency had? Did she sell those to Linc, too? And if so, why hadn't the police found them when they must have searched Linc's belongings? Where could he have been keeping them?

There were just too many questions to find answers for tonight.

"We appreciate your coming by to tell us all this, Finn," Sander said. "Gives us a lot to think about. We do want to keep up with any developments in Linc's case."

The others nodded their agreement, but no one said anything more. Roth told Finn he'd see him out, and Finn lifted a hand in silent farewell, his gaze moving from one Fortune to another before finally settling on Zara and staying there.

"It was good to see you, Zara," he said softly.

She looked a little stricken by the comment but forced a smile. "You, too, Finn," she said just as quietly.

With one last long look, Finn turned back to the kitchen entrance, and Roth followed. At the front door, Finn reiterated his apologies for the interruption and his thanks for their time, then headed for the sleek, low-slung car in the drive. As Roth closed the door behind him, he remembered Sander's words about turning adversity into prosperity. Finn Morrison had clearly done exactly that. If the oil executive was trying to merge his company with one in Abu Dhabi, he'd definitely risen above his humble roots on the wrong side of the Emerald Ridge tracks.

And then that thought was gone, and his brain began to buzz with everything he'd learned about Linc Banning tonight. His family was buzzing, too, when he got back to the patio, all talking at once about what could possibly be going on with their old friend.

When there was a break in the chatter, Sander said, "It sure would be helpful if our cousins Drake and Cameron were in town so we could ask them more about Courtney Wellington and everything she did."

The other Fortunes murmured their agreement. Unfortunately, the newly reunited twin brothers were both out of the country on what was going to be a months-long business trip to a million different cities in Europe. And they'd taken Drake's fiancée, Annelise Wellington—Courtney's stepdaughter, who'd been as in the dark about her stepmother's actions as everyone else in town—with them. There was little chance any of them would have a chance to talk to the other Fortunes anytime soon, since they were all going to be pretty much impossible to reach.

"So all we can do is speculate," Sander said flatly.

"And hope the police get to the bottom of things soon."

The sooner, the better, Roth thought. They all wanted to see justice done for Linc Banning. Not to mention they all needed to get back to their lives outside of Emerald Ridge.

He waited for the worry and concern to wash over him that normally accompanied thoughts about how long he'd been away from the office. Funny, though, how neither of those things came. He told himself it was because he was too busy puzzling over everything Finn had revealed to them tonight. But it wasn't Finn he was thinking about just then. It was Antonia. And little Georgie. And just the simple thought of those two appearing in his brain chased away any fears or concerns he had about work. Or the investigation into Linc's murder. Yes, he still had concerns about both. But those worries didn't seem as overwhelming as they had a few weeks ago. Being away from work wasn't the end of the world. Things at Fortune Capital had been moving along just fine this month, even with him out of town. And he was confident that Linc's killer would eventually be brought to justice.

He thought about Antonia again, about the sizzle of heat that wound through him when she kissed him on her front porch. And about how good it had felt to wake up in his bed and find her there beside him. How could they have thought either of those things was a mistake? They'd felt like the most natural thing in the world when they happened. And, suddenly, Roth wanted them to happen again. And again.

And again.

He looked at his family, still engrossed in Finn's revelations and what it could all mean, and he marveled— not for the first time—at how lucky he was to have them as family. But that was the thing about family...there was always room for more.

"Hey, you guys," he called out to the other Fortunes.

They all stopped talking and looked at him.

He started backing toward the sliding door to the kitchen. "I need to go out for a little while."

They all threw him curious looks. "Go out where?" Harris asked. "Emerald Ridge is going to be rolling up the sidewalks before long."

"Yeah, well, I'm not going into town."

Priscilla smiled that same knowing smile she'd had the morning he overheard Charles Cabot badmouthing Antonia and Roth declared his need to defend her. "Then where *are* you going, big brother?"

"I just need to, um, see to a matter."

Kelsey smiled, too. "What kind of matter?" she asked. "A matter of the heart maybe?"

Roth started to deny it, then figured he'd probably be better off saying nothing at all. Still walking backward, he bumped into the sliding door and reached for the handle, pushing one side open. "I'll be back in a little while," he said as he stepped through.

He did his best to close the door again before anyone could ask him anything else. But he wasn't quick enough to avoid hearing Priscilla say, "Tell Antonia we all said hi!"

Chapter Eleven

Antonia was getting Georgie ready for bed when the front doorbell rang downstairs, a sound that just made her feel more irritable than she already was. Except for Papa, she was the only one home, so she would have to be the one to answer it and deal with whatever it was. Gia was in Mexico, touring a vineyard with their mother along for the ride, and Bella and the kids had gone to a concert at the park. As quickly as she could, she finished snapping Georgie into her daisy-spattered sleeper and headed them both downstairs, silently rehearsing the list of things she had to do the next day. Make a grocery run, take Georgie to look for new shoes now that she was walking more—though still hanging on to the furniture when she did—pick up her blouse from the dry-cleaner and hope they got out all the stains from the birthday party, and—

And then completely losing her train of thought when she opened the front door to find Roth Fortune standing on the other side.

"Hey," he said softly.

"Hey," she replied just as quietly.

And that was the entirety of their conversation for

a moment. Antonia had honestly forgotten how handsome he was. As many times as she had replayed their last night and morning together in her head—and she had replayed that a *lot* over the last week—the image of him in her mind was nowhere near as breathtaking as the reality. Even in the pale light of the dying day, his blue eyes shone like aquamarine, and his dark hair was kissed with threads of gold. His pale blue Western shirt strained against his broad shoulders, making her want to reach out and unbutton it the way she had that night at his house, before tracing her fingers over the elegant muscles of his torso. He was holding his Stetson in both hands—hands that had been so gentle and sensual caressing her naked skin—and he was nervously turning it at its brim. It was all she could do not to lean forward and cover his mouth with hers, to kiss him with all the passion and need and desire and—

"Rah," Georgie sang out happily, interrupting the silence that had fallen over them.

It took a moment for the word to register with Antonia, but when it did, her eyes widened, and she looked at her daughter in astonishment. "What did you just say?" she asked the little girl.

"Rah," Georgie repeated. And then, just in case her mother didn't already understand what she was talking about, the baby pointed at Roth and repeated, "Rah."

Now Antonia looked at Roth, who seemed oblivious to what was happening. "Did you hear that?" she asked. "Georgie just said your name. She called you 'Roth.'"

His dark eyebrows shot up, then he looked at the baby, too. Georgie laughed and reached out both arms toward him. Then, even more clearly than before, she said, "Hi, Rah."

At this, Antonia's mouth dropped open. "She put two words together. She said, 'Hi, Roth.' She's never done that before. This is a huge milestone!"

Roth looked a little overwhelmed by the announcement. Then he grinned from ear to ear. Georgie still had her pudgy little arms outstretched toward him and was now wiggling her fingers in the *Want it now* gesture Antonia recognized too well. He must have understood it, too, because he settled his hat on his head and lifted his own arms toward the baby. Carefully, he took Georgie from Antonia, arranging the little girl easily against his chest. The second he did, Georgie grabbed his nose and squeezed it, laughing with delight. Roth chuckled, too, and, just like that, the sadness and gloom that had been Antonia's companions all week disappeared, and her laughter joined theirs.

"This is amazing," she said. "First Georgie takes her first steps the other day, then she's putting words together." She met Roth's gaze levelly. With a soft smile she just couldn't help, she added softly, "And now you've shown up at my front door."

The happiness that welled up inside her was almost more than she could bear. This week had been the hardest one Antonia had ever had to get through. Worse than the ones after discovering Silvio had been cheating on her for years. Or after discovering Charles had only planned to marry her for her money. Worse, even, than those long endless nights when Georgie had gone through colic when she was a month old, because she'd known that, eventually, her daughter would be fine. This week, however, Antonia had thought she and Roth were parted for good, and she'd wondered if anything in her life would ever be fine again.

Georgie removed her hand from his nose and patted his jaw. "Rah," she murmured again before snuggling more closely against him.

Antonia was stunned. Touching a person's cheek that way was how Georgie showed affection to others. And although she'd certainly known since day one that her daughter liked Roth, she truly hadn't realized how much. What Georgie was showing him now was *love*. Not that that should surprise her. Because Antonia had begun to realize she might be in love with Roth, too. She just wished she could trust her feelings as much as Georgie obviously trusted her own.

"I've missed you, too, li'l cowgirl," Roth said softly as he looked down at the baby. Then his gaze connected with Antonia's. "And I've missed you, Antonia," he added. "A lot."

She was about to blurt that she had missed him more than he could ever know but stopped herself. The truth was she still didn't know if what she was feeling was an honest reaction or the result of feeling too much of everything else over the past month. Bottom line? She still didn't trust herself to know what was best for her and her daughter. But she knew she needed to say *something*. Because Roth was looking at her now as if her silence was breaking his heart.

"Look, I know we kind of agreed not to see each other again," he hurried on, "but we never really said that out loud. And I know you need your space, and I know I should give it to you. But we never said that out loud, either." Now his dark brows arrowed down in dismay. "I miss you, Antonia. I feel awful when you're not around. I don't want there to be space between us."

She swallowed hard. "I don't want that either," she finally said.

But she didn't know what else to do. She still wasn't sure if she could trust her heart. There were times when she still wasn't sure what her feelings even were. Part of her knew she was in love with Roth Fortune. But another part kept reminding her about how wrong she'd been before. There was one thing, though, of which she was absolutely certain. She didn't want Roth to leave. Like, ever.

"Do you want to come in?" she asked impulsively. "Obviously, you and I need to talk. And Georgie's nowhere close to being sleepy. Maybe the fun of having you here will wear her out some."

And maybe having him here would help Antonia sort through her confusion.

"I'd love to," he said.

She held up her hands to Georgie, to tempt her back into her mother's embrace, but the baby shook her head and leaned into Roth instead.

"I don't mind," he said, tightening his hold on the little girl. "I promise I won't drop her."

Antonia wasn't worried about that. She was worried that Georgie was never going to let him go. The same way she didn't ever want to let him go, either. She opened the door wider and took a few steps back, and Roth crossed the threshold. He followed her up the stairs, back to the room across from the nursery that they'd occupied that first night he was here. Once inside, Georgie allowed him to set her down, and she immediately crawled to the corner Antonia had filled with toys for her daughter to play with whenever she worked from home in here. Roth removed his Stetson again and set it on a chair, then took his seat on the sofa where he'd sat that first night.

Had that really been less than a month ago? Antonia could scarcely believe it. She felt as if she'd lived two lifetimes since then.

"Wine?" she asked. Because she, for one, could use a little something to calm down the butterflies that were doing a crazy mambo inside her.

Roth nodded. "Please." Just from that one word, she could tell that his nerves were pretty raucous, too.

She didn't even bother to look at what she withdrew from the rack, grabbing the opener with the other hand and jamming it into the cork. Twist, twist, twist, *pop*, then *splish splash* into the glasses. Instead of sitting in the chair opposite him as she had that first night, after handing Roth his glass, Antonia folded herself next to him on the sofa. Their gazes met and, with a soft smile, Antonia lifted her glass. Roth tapped his against hers with a soft *clink*, and they both drank. She had no idea what they were toasting. But they seemed to be commemorating something that had happened. Or maybe celebrating something that was about to start. Something good. Something she hoped they would both figure out at some point and be able to celebrate more often. Maybe even regularly.

Hey, a girl could dream.

She closed her eyes as she swallowed her wine in an effort to help the warmth of the velvety liquid winding through her settle her apprehension. When she opened them again, it was to find Roth gazing at her face intently.

"What?" she asked.

He shook his head almost imperceptibly. "It's just good to see you. It's been a crummy week. And I was starting to worry we might never sit like this again."

She nodded. "I haven't had such a great week, either."

"But Georgie had two big milestones. You said so yourself."

"Yeah, Georgie has had a wonderful week. Me, not so much."

"Why not?"

She hesitated. Then she made herself tell him the truth. "I'm worried I made a huge mistake."

He hesitated a moment, then gave her a soft, teasing smile. "Yeah, I was wondering why I didn't receive a new proposal from you this week."

She smiled back. "I've had a lot on my mind. But I'm not talking about that mistake. I'm talking about a different one. A much bigger, much worse one."

His smile fell some. "And what mistake was that?"

Be honest, she told herself again. "The really colossally bad one. The one I made about us."

Had she thought he looked heartbroken before? Because he looked way worse than that now. Then she realized he thought she meant the mistake she'd made about them was making love at his house last weekend, which wasn't the case at all. The mistake she'd made was calling it quits with Roth. At the time, it had seemed like the right thing—the only thing—she could do. Now, though, she just wasn't sure.

Before she could tell him all that, he said, a little hopefully, she couldn't help thinking, "Well, that's the good thing about mistakes. They can usually be fixed."

She knew that was true. But she just had no idea how to go about fixing this one. Should she and Roth try to work things out? Or would doing that just lead to an even more disastrous breakup than before? One she might never recover from? It wasn't like there was a clear way for them to work this out. No black and white. No wrong or right. No bottom line. Just lots of shades of gray and lots of *ifs*, *ands* and *buts*. How was she supposed to know if what she was feeling for Roth was something that would last?

It wasn't like she had a crystal ball that would show her his heart and his mind and how the future would turn out for them. She'd spent a third of her life—her entire adult life—believing in people who had let her down. Not just let her down. Who had betrayed her. And now she could very well be rushing headlong into the arms of another one.

How could she trust herself to know what was what?

Then again, it wasn't just herself she needed to trust, she realized. She needed to trust Roth, too.

Antonia smiled when the thought took hold. Because she knew she already did trust him. She wouldn't have made love with him the way they had, and she wouldn't be sitting here with him—and Georgie—now if she didn't already know he was an honorable man. A man she could depend on. A man who loved her, too. She did trust Roth. Which meant, hey, she was already halfway where she needed to be.

Roth seemed to understand the tumultuous feelings cartwheeling through her head, because he set his wine-glass on the table beside the sofa and took her free hand in his. Then he opened her fingers and turned her palm upward, lifting it to his mouth for a soft kiss. A ribbon of something sweet and sensuous wound through her at the touch. Even that simple gesture made her feel as if nothing in the world could go wrong again.

He wove their fingers together and drew them to his chest, settling them against his heart. "Look, Antonia, I don't want to lose you," he said without preamble and with absolute certainty. "I've never met anyone like you, and I've never felt about anyone else the way I feel about you." When she didn't reply right away—mostly because she didn't trust the words that might come out of her mouth—he continued, "And call me crazy, but I think you might kind of like me, too."

She smiled at that. "I do like you. I like you a lot. I—" *No, don't use the L-word*, she told herself. Even if she was truly beginning to believe she had indeed fallen in love with Roth Fortune—she shouldn't say the words out loud. Every time she'd told a man she loved him, that man had turned on her. Maybe if she didn't say it this time…

It was a lame reason, she reminded herself. But she

was still afraid to say it. So she only echoed, "I do like you, Roth. More than you could possibly know."

As ambivalent as she thought the words sounded, they obviously heartened him. A lot. "Then I'm hoping you also feel the same way I do about not wanting to call it quits on whatever this thing is that's been going on between us."

She didn't want to call it quits on that. But she was still afraid of what might happen if they continued. Even so, she confessed, "I don't. But how are we supposed to keep it up? You live in Dallas, I live here. You've said yourself how important your work is to you. And your family. My work and family are important to me, too. And my whole life is here in Emerald Ridge. So is Georgie's."

She didn't bother reminding him about how he'd also confided to her that first night how he would be a terrible father. It had become obvious to both of them by now that that wasn't true at all. Still, a child was a huge responsibility that even people who liked children didn't always want to take on. There was no reason to think Roth *wanted* to be a father.

Somehow, he read her mind, anyway. "I don't want to lose you *or* Georgie," he told her. "I know I said that first day that I didn't think I'd be a good father to anyone. But being around your daughter has changed my mind. I'd like to see how that plays out, too. I can't promise I won't make mistakes—with you or with Georgie—but I'd like to see where this takes us."

"It will take you to Dallas and leave me in Emerald Ridge," she said softly, since he hadn't addressed that part. "We can't see how this plays out when we're both living separate lives in different cities."

"Dallas is only an hour away," he reminded her. "Hell, that's a morning commute for a lot of people in this country."

"So who's going to be the one driving back and forth?" she asked him. "You or me?"

He didn't reply right away. But he didn't look like he was worried about the answer, either. He was right. An hour wasn't that long. But they really did lead two different lives that were both full and complicated. She couldn't just pack up a baby whenever she wanted and take off. And if this thing between them lasted years, her daughter would be starting school one day. Then Antonia and Georgie both would be bound to Emerald Ridge by obligations. Roth couldn't exactly just up and leave behind a billion-dollar business he'd built and nurtured on his own, one that needed to be in a huge financial hub. Which Emerald Ridge most certainly was not.

Finally, Antonia said what needed to be said. "One of us is going to have to make some huge sacrifices if we're going to make this work."

He nodded at that. "I know. I realize it's going to take a lot of planning and organization and patience to do it. And it won't happen overnight. But it can work, Antonia. It *will* work. If you and I just give ourselves time to figure it all out. God knows I'm willing to do that if you are."

Time. Maybe it really did all come down to that. Antonia knew she loved Roth. She knew he was a good guy. She knew he loved her and Georgie both—she could feel it. But that knowledge and those feelings were still tangled up with so many other feelings, too. One of which was still the fear that things might not work out for some other reason. It was one thing to risk her own heart. But she'd be putting her daughter's heart on the line, too. Could she do that?

As if Georgie could sense the turmoil eating Antonia up inside, she cried out from the corner, "Mama! Rah!"

Antonia and Roth both looked in that direction to find that Georgie had hauled herself up to standing and was clinging to the top of a dollhouse, steadying herself with one hand. Instinctively, Antonia rose to go to her, worried her daughter would take a spill if she wasn't careful. Before she could reach Georgie, though, the little girl released the dollhouse and took a single, unsteady step forward, all by herself.

Antonia's heart leaped to her throat. Her baby had just taken her first step alone!

She hurried to Georgie's side just as her daughter took another, this time less unsteady, step forward. Then another. By the time Antonia reached her, Georgie was on her way, taking one slow, ponderous step after another. But she didn't stop for her mother. She walked right past her. Feeling only a tiny bit slighted, Antonia followed behind her daughter as she took a half dozen steps more, toward Roth.

Roth, who dropped from the couch to both knees on the floor, arms outstretched toward the little girl, with all the delight of a proud father. Georgie took three more steps forward, then launched herself into his arms with a laugh. Roth laughed, too, as he hugged her close.

"Look at you go!" he said to the joyful toddler. Because after this, Georgie could officially be called a toddler. "Nothing's gonna stop you now!"

Nothing *would* stop Georgie now, Antonia knew. Her
daughter had just taken the first independent steps of a
lifetime. It would all be different from here on out. For
both of them. She wouldn't be able to take an eye off her
toddler for a moment now that her baby girl was on the
move. Soon, it wouldn't just be walking and talking she
was mastering. Soon—too soon—she would be learning
all kinds of things. How to skip and jump. How to read.
How to make her own friends. How to think for herself.
Someday, she would even leave home and go to college.
And eventually, she would start a life of her own.

Meaning Antonia would be completely removed from
the equation. She was just going to have to trust that
her little girl would make good decisions as her life un-
folded.

There was that word again. *Trust.* As Antonia
watched Roth with her daughter, so gentle, so sweet,
so loving, she realized he was nothing like the men she'd
allowed into her life before. He would never betray her.
Or her daughter. He would never put his own interests
or needs ahead of theirs the way Silvio and Charles had.
He would keep his word and do whatever he had to do
to make sure that what the two of them had discovered
together over the last few weeks *would* work out. Forever. Because he was willing to make the necessary
sacrifices that would make them a family. She truly did
love him for that. And for so many other reasons. And

she knew in that moment that she would love him forever. She *knew* that. She trusted that.

She was about to tell him so when he scooped up Georgie and began to dance her around the room, telling her how someday she was going to be an Olympic marathon runner or a champion ballroom dancer. Then he looked over at Antonia.

"Or maybe," he told the little girl, "you'll be a high-falutin CFO like your mom. Just be sure that now that you've started walking, you'll keep moving forward and never look back."

Keep moving forward, Antonia repeated to herself. *Never look back.* Sage advice indeed. She'd spent the last month living in the past, berating herself for all the things she'd done wrong. Maybe it was time to start looking forward to the future and doing some things right.

Yeah. That was exactly what she should do.

She covered the distance between Roth and her daughter, both of whom never took their eyes off her as she did. When she arrived at their side, she curled one arm over Georgie's back and looped the other around Roth's waist. Still holding the toddler close, Roth leaned in to brush his lips lightly over Antonia's, once, twice, three times, the same way he had the first time he kissed her. And just like that time, Antonia's heart beat faster, her blood raced through her veins and her entire body grew warm. When she finally pulled away, Georgie lifted both hands, placing one on Antonia's cheek and the other on Roth's. As if she were giving them both her approval for whatever lay ahead.

And there was a lot that lay ahead. Antonia had no idea what the particulars were, but for the first time in a long time, she couldn't wait to find out what the future held. For all of them.

"I love you, Roth Fortune," she said without a trace of doubt.

He looked a little surprised for a moment, then he smiled. "I love you, too, Antonia Leonetti."

"We have a lot to talk about," she told him.

"Yeah, we do," he agreed.

"And we have all the time in the world to do it."

"However long it takes," Roth promised. "I'll be there, Antonia. You set the pace. I'm not going anywhere."

Epilogue

Spring came slowly to Emerald Ridge sometimes, and this was just such a year. Not that Roth had a lot of experience with springtime here, since he'd mostly spent the summer months at his family's home. But Antonia had mentioned the weather on a fairly regular basis over the last nine months, mostly in reference to the progress of the grapes. As he looked out over the expanse of the Fortune's Vintages vineyard on the outskirts of Emerald Ridge, however, things looked just fine to him. The buds on the vines had broken in early April, and tiny white flowers had formed on the shoots soon after.

Now, in mid-May, the grapes were doing very well. There had been just enough rain over the winter, and no particularly inclement weather to hinder their growth, something that could make or break an entire year's worth of cultivation. As summer set in, the flowers would shed their petals, allowing clusters of grapes to start forming. After that, with a little more time, their colors would begin to show, either the rich blues and purples of the red varieties or the greens and yellows of the whites.

He and Antonia, too, had come a long way since both

their vineyards had harvested their grapes last fall. But where their vineyards' fields had lain dormant all winter, their relationship had been anything but. It seemed as if with every new month, they learned something about each other they hadn't known before, or they discovered something they had in common that they hadn't previously realized. By now, they were about as comfortable together as a couple could be. But they never stopped looking toward the future.

He looked over at her now, seated beside him on the patio of the Fortune's Vintages tasting room, a building that looked more like a Craftsman-style home than a business fixture. It was Sunday, so the vineyard was pretty much deserted, but he'd wanted to swing by and sample the burgundy they'd be releasing in a matter of weeks. He and Antonia and Georgie had spent the day at Emerald Ridge Park, feeding the ducks at the duck pond and giving the playground a run for its money.

Roth had spent nearly as much time here since the beginning of the year as he'd spent in Dallas. And Antonia and Georgie had spent nearly as much time with him at his place as they had here. The high-rise condo he'd always thought so soulless and sterile was now cluttered with the remnants of the mingling of their lives. The room that had been his media room—not that he'd ever used any of the media in there—was now Georgie's bedroom, teeming with toys and color.

He'd redone one of the bedrooms at his house here in Emerald Ridge for her, too, so that Antonia wouldn't have to leave her with a sitter on the nights she spent at his place. He'd even gone so far as to hire a local artist

to turn one of the walls into a mural of Leonetti Vineyards, though it was painted to look like the backdrop
of a Disney film, right down to the little fairies and en-
chanted baby animals cavorting around the vines. Yeah,
he could have had the artist paint Fortune's Vintages
instead, or even meld both businesses into one image
that represented them both. But hey, there were three
other walls in there to paint with other scenes someday.
Like, say…oh, he didn't know…maybe Fortune's Vintages. The very sight he and Antonia were enjoying now.

The three of them had spent today the same way they
had nearly every weekend since he and Antonia admitted their feelings, both to each other and to themselves,
last August—being together, doing whatever. Over the
last few seasons, they'd done everything from hitting
the pool at Fortune's Gold Guest Ranch to hiking at
Emerald Ridge Hot Spring to seeing *Winnie the Pooh*
at Retro Reels, the town's revival house movie theater.
The kinds of things families did all the time, he couldn't
help thinking. Probably because, even without realizing
it, the three of them *had* become a family.

Unofficially, at least. And even though he'd been
ready to marry Antonia on the spot last August, he knew
she'd needed time. Yes, she trusted both her feelings and
him—their love had only become stronger with every
passing day—but she'd wanted to take things slowly, so
that they could grow into both the couple and family
they had ultimately become. Taking things slowly had
been totally okay with Roth, though. As far as he was
concerned, they had all the time in the world.

Antonia was leaning back in her chair with her face

turned toward the dying sunlight, her eyes closed, as if to better enjoy the music of the evening breeze and Georgie's laughter as the little girl buzzed around the patio. The toddler had taken Roth's advice to heart that day she took her first steps and hadn't slowed down for a moment.

"Happy?" he asked Antonia before he could stop himself.

Without opening her eyes, she nodded. "Oh, yes."

"It was a good day, huh?"

"One of the best."

"But we didn't do anything out of the ordinary."

She opened her eyes and smiled at him. "That's what made it so great. That we can do nothing, as long as we're all together, and it's still the best day ever. Tomorrow will be even better."

Roth smiled, too. "Why? What are we doing tomorrow?"

She closed her eyes again and sighed. "The exact same thing."

Yeah, that sounded pretty good to him, too.

Georgie suddenly erupted in laughter at something only a twenty-month-old could appreciate—which, admittedly, could be just about anything. The little girl had doubled in size since he'd first met her. Her dark hair was long enough now that Antonia had gathered it today atop her head in a scrunchie made from the same fabric as the strawberry-spattered romper she was wearing. Roth congratulated himself on remembering that such a garment and accessory were called a romper and a scrunchie respectively. He'd learned all kinds of things about toddler paraphernalia since last summer. He could throw around words like *teether* and *boogie wipes* and *sippy cup* with absolute confidence these days.

As if the little girl—she was most definitely a little girl now, not a little baby—had heard his thoughts, she stopped poking whatever had caught her fascination in one of the potted plants, her gaze moving from him to Antonia and back to him again. Then she smiled. That four-toothed smile that always made something inside him turn into a little puddle of goo.

"Dah pay wit Joe Gee?" she asked. "Wee boo? Foe bah?"

Translation, *Da play with Georgie? Read book? Throw ball?* He understood every word. Especially that first one, which was another thing that turned his insides into mush. At some point over the last nine months, Georgie's use of "Rah" for him had turned into "Dah." As in *Da*. As in the short form of *Dada*. As in something that might someday even turn into the longer form of *Daddy*.

He pushed the thought to the back of his brain as he always did when it formed. Yes, he and Antonia had come a long way in nine months, but they were still in motion. They'd kept their promise to take things slow, and it still hadn't been a year since her split with Cabot. And while they'd talked about a future together, they'd never actually used any words like *commitment*. Even so, they were totally committed. They were practically living together now, both in Emerald Ridge and in Dallas, though Roth did officially stay at his place on the Fortune compound when he was here. During the day, anyway. Nights, they kind of switched back and forth, but they always parted ways in the morning to return to their individual homes and lives. He was getting tired of that daily parting, though. He wanted to be with Antonia all the time, the two of them together in both a home and a life. He just wasn't sure when she would be ready for that.

He was about to tell the little girl that he'd be delighted to *wee* her whatever *boo* was in the toddler bag Antonia had packed that morning, but her mother answered first.

"Dah can read to you later, sweetie," she told her daughter. "Mommy needs to talk to Dah about something first."

"Okay," Georgie replied agreeably.

She went to the corner of the patio to inspect another plant, her entire attention focused on the ficus. Roth shook his head. If there was one thing he'd learned about little ones, it was that they were fascinated by *everything*. There were times, like when he watched Georgie catch a newly fallen leaf or traced raindrops on a window, when he could almost hear the synapses in her brain crackling into a new connection.

"She never seems to get tired of discovering new things," he said.

"I hope she stays that way forever," Antonia replied. Then she turned to Roth. "And speaking about new things, I have a new proposal for you."

He sighed inwardly. Here they went again. One thing that hadn't changed over the last nine months was the Leonettis' desire to acquire Fortune's Vintages. Although Antonia had cooled it for the most part, he knew her brother, Leo, and her sister Bella especially still wanted to get their hands on his grapes—and his clients. His harvest last fall had been an especially good one, the grapes promising to produce some extremely good wine.

"Can we talk about this another time?" he asked. "I mean, it's been such a nice day with Georgie and all, and I'd—"

"No, I think you're going to want to hear this proposal," she said.

"The last proposal Gia and Leo put together was in no way tempting," Roth reminded her.

"Gia and Leo had nothing to do with this one," she assured him. "This one is coming from me and me alone."

Roth eyed her warily.

"It's a really good proposal," she promised.

That remained to be seen. If CFO Antonia was proposing something, then it was all going to come down to money. Which, okay, Roth liked money a lot—hell, he made most of his money with money—but that wasn't necessarily a deciding factor for a business like winemaking. Especially since winemaking was becoming more to him than a business. Still, he knew Antonia well enough to know she wasn't going to stop until he listened to her *really good proposal*. So he would listen to it, tell her he still wasn't interested, and then they could move along with their evening.

"Okay, fine," he relented. "I'll listen to this one."

For a moment, she said nothing, only studied him in the lavender light of the oncoming evening. Somewhere in the distance, a prairie falcon cried out, while, closer by, Georgie began to softly sing. He smiled when he recognized her murmurs as "Moon River." Or, as the little girl sang it, "Moo Wibbon." It was a song he sang to her at night because his mother had sung it to him.

He waited for Antonia to withdraw one of her ubiquitous blue folders from thin air. But tonight, there was no blue folder. There was only the woman he loved, biting her lip thoughtfully, as if she were trying very hard to figure out how to say what she wanted to say. Hmm. Maybe this time she really was going to offer him the moon.

Finally, she said, "Since you've never accepted a Leonetti proposal before, I'm just going to bring this one down to the bottom line."

Roth nodded his approval. "I like bottom lines. There's no negotiating with a bottom line."

"Well, there's still going to have to be a bit of negotiating," she told him. Before he could ask for clarification on that, she hurried on, "But here's the bottom line. Roth Fortune, will you marry me?"

Certain he must have misheard, he stammered, "Wh-what?"

She grinned. "Will you marry me? It's a good proposal."

Was she kidding? It was the best proposal he'd ever had from anyone. She really was offering him the moon.

"Are you sure you're ready?" he asked her. Not that he wanted her to change her mind or anything. He just really did want her to be sure.

She grinned. "If there's one thing I've learned over

the last nine months, it's that I was ready nine months ago. I've never been more sure of anything in my life than I am of you. Of us. Of…" She sighed happily. "Of everything. I love you, Roth Fortune. More than I've ever loved anyone. In a way that I've never loved anyone. And I want you to marry me. So will you?"

He grinned. "You're damned right I will."

"Even though you live in Dallas, and I live here?"

"Antonia, I think it's become pretty clear by now that the two of us can do just about anything from just about anywhere. When I need to go into Dallas, it's only an hour away. We both have strong ties to Emerald Ridge. And it'll be a great place to raise our family." After a moment's pause, he added, "And to add to it. If that's what you want, too."

"I do," she said softly.

He laughed lightly at her wording. "I do, too."

Antonia laughed with him. Then they both stood and embraced, their mouths locking in a kiss to seal the deal. Before they could go too far, though—time enough for that later, Roth thought—they pulled away enough to lock their gazes instead. Georgie must have sensed something major was happening, because she toddled over to where they were standing and wrapped both arms tightly around their legs.

Roth looked down at the little girl, then back up at Antonia. "Uh-oh. Looks like we're gonna be stuck together for a while," he said.

"Forever," Antonia assured him.

"Foehbah," Georgie echoed.

He grinned. "Look at that. Another new word to add to Georgie's list."

"It's a good word," Antonia said.

"One of the best," he agreed.

And it was a word Roth knew all three of them would be using a lot from here on out. Yeah, they were going to be using that one…forever.

* * * * *

Don't miss the next installment of the new continuity
The Fortunes of Texas: Fortune's Hidden Treasures
Fortune's Fake Marriage Plan
by USA TODAY *bestselling author*
Tara Taylor Quinn

On sale September 2025,
wherever Harlequin books and ebooks are sold.

Harlequin® Reader Service

Enjoyed your book?

Try the perfect subscription for Romance readers and get more great books like this delivered right to your door.

See why over 10+ million readers have tried Harlequin Reader Service.

Start with a Free Welcome Collection with free books and a gift—valued over $20.

Choose any series in print or ebook. See website for details and order today:

TryReaderService.com/subscriptions

RSBPA2409

Harlequin Reader Service

Enjoyed your book?

Start with a Free Welcome
Collection with free books and
a gift—valued at over $20

Try Readerservice.com/subscribe